Giada had h  **minions, jus** **time before s**

Because even a w .... phone call with Gigi and agreeing to this mad ploy, Giada had known she wasn't ready.

Exhibit one—the way she'd greet him.

She'd forgotten to ask Gigi how to address the imposing, dynamic man looking down at her with hooded eyes, disdain dripping from every bronzed, polished pore on his body.

With every bone in her body, she yearned to turned away from that judgmental stare.

But she'd promised her sister she would do whatever it took to buy time for Gigi to rectify her mistake. She couldn't let her down at the first hurdle.

Her heart jumped when Alessio's eyes shifted back to her and narrowed.

God, had she given herself away already?

Swallowing, she went for broke, strode forward on precariously spindly high heels, and resting her hands on his arms, she raised herself on tiptoe and brushed a kiss across Alessio Montaldi's cheek.

"I didn't know you were in town."

His jaw rippled, his gaze fixated on her when she took a vital step back. "Did you not?"

Hot Winter Escapes

Sun, snow and sexy seductions...

Whether it's a trip to the Swiss Alps or a rendezvous on a gorgeous Hawaiian beach, warming up in front of the fire or basking in the sizzling sun, these billion-dollar getaways provide the perfect backdrops for even more scorching winter romances and passionately-ever-afters!

Escape to some winter sun in...

Bound by Her Baby Revelation by Cathy Williams

An Heir Made in Hawaii by Emmy Grayson

Claimed by the Crown Prince by Abby Green

One Forbidden Night in Paradise by Louise Fuller

And get cozy in these luxurious snowy hideaways...

A Nine-Month Deal with Her Husband
by Joss Wood

Snowbound with the Irresistible Sicilian
by Maya Blake

Undoing His Innocent Enemy
by Heidi Rice

In Bed with Her Billionaire Bodyguard
by Pippa Roscoe

All available now!

Maya Blake

SNOWBOUND WITH THE IRRESISTIBLE SICILIAN

Recycling programs
for this product may
not exist in your area.

ISBN-13: 978-1-335-59315-3

Snowbound with the Irresistible Sicilian

Copyright © 2023 by Maya Blake

Harlequin Enterprises ULC
22 Adelaide St. West, 41st Floor
Toronto, Ontario M5H 4E3, Canada
www.Harlequin.com

Printed in U.S.A.

Maya Blake's hopes of becoming a writer were born when she picked up her first romance at thirteen. Little did she know her dream would come true! Does she still pinch herself every now and then to make sure it's not a dream? Yes, she does! Feel free to pinch her, too, via Twitter, Facebook or Goodreads! Happy reading!

Books by Maya Blake

Harlequin Presents

Reclaimed for His Royal Bed
The Greek's Forgotten Marriage
Pregnant and Stolen by the Tycoon

Brothers of the Desert

Their Desert Night of Scandal
His Pregnant Desert Queen

Ghana's Most Eligible Billionaires

Bound by Her Rival's Baby
A Vow to Claim His Hidden Son

Visit the Author Profile page
at Harlequin.com for more titles.

CHAPTER ONE

DR GIADA PARKER clutched her travel coffee mug, her eyes stinging a little as the Antarctic wind picked up speed and whipped across her face.

She smiled through the discomfort.

Her triple-insulated weather gear protected her from the worst of the freezing temperatures, and, if needed, she could retreat to the significantly less chilly staff quarters below deck of the research vessel she'd called home for the last four months.

This was her last chance to see this intensely breath-taking landscape before her stint was officially over and she wasn't about to miss it.

She sipped her coffee, welcoming the scalding heat but not the reminder of what awaited her back home in London. Or Rome. Or wherever her mother decided they would spend Christmas this year. As of their last, terse conversation a month ago, Renata DiMarco hadn't decided where she would be dragging Giada and her identical twin sister to for the festivities.

With every bone in her body, Giada wished she could be spared the ordeal. Perhaps it was blasphemy to admit it, but Christmas wasn't her favourite time of year. Hell, she'd go as far as to say she detested it. Too many occasions over the years filled with too many harrowing scenes of Renata acting out after the inevitable several glasses of champagne had ruined the holiday for her. Her sister, Gigi, had weathered the storms better than she had, but then hadn't their mother accused Giada of being too sensitive, *too square*, among her many sins?

'You should be more like your sister. She knows how to enjoy life...'

That particular piece of unsolicited advice had been given when she'd sent her mother an invitation to her graduation. Predictably, Renata DiMarco had found somewhere else to be as her daughter had earned her PhD in marine biology.

Giada had assured herself she didn't care that neither Gigi nor her mother had made it or that the father she could barely remember hadn't even bothered to RSVP. But the thorns of anguish in her heart as she'd walked across the stage to collect her certificate had labelled her a liar.

She took another sip, more to calm her jangling nerves than for warmth. Staring across the blinding-white frozen tundra, she made a half-hearted wish for deliverance.

Then laughed in nervous shock as the vessel lurched, forcing her to reach for the railing to steady herself.

A warning that she shouldn't tempt fate, perhaps?

She snorted under her breath.

Yeah, right. Fate had a habit of ignoring her most ardent wishes. Giada was sure she wasn't about to start granting them now.

The only guaranteed thing was that she would at

least get a few days' respite in her London bedsit before the summons from Renata arrived. A few days to shore up her emotional defences against the parent who didn't see anything wrong with denigrating her at every opportunity—

'Giada?'

She turned her head, startled to see Martin, her boss, standing a short distance away wearing a concerned frown.

'I'm sorry, Martin, I was miles away. Did you want something?'

The frown dissipated and a smile peeked through his months' old beard. 'I was a little worried you'd turned into a statue, you were so still. Anyway, you got a call five minutes ago. Your sister? I came to get you. She's calling back in ten.'

A ripple of anxiety washed over her.

In the four months she'd been away she'd spoken to her sister three times, all calls Giada had initiated, not the other way around. Gigi habitually forgot she had a twin for weeks at a stretch, and, while Giada knew it was extreme absent-mindedness coupled with the hard partying her influencer sister indulged in, it occasionally sharpened that same pang of unhappiness Giada had lived with for most of her life.

'Did she say what it was about?' she asked Martin, her stomach tightening involuntarily as she followed him across the snow-covered deck to the stairs leading to the lower levels.

He shook his head. 'She didn't. If it's helpful, she didn't sound like something was wrong.' He flashed a reassuring smile and gestured for her to precede him down the stairs. 'It sounded like she was in a bar, actually. God, I'd give my arm for a pint in a warm pub right now.'

She smiled but didn't bother to tell him Gigi would sound laid-back in the middle of a blazing apocalypse. Giada used to envy her sister's ability to remain unflappable in the face of their mother's melodramatic tantrums and the resulting angst-filled days Giada had endured.

Now, as she hurried after Martin, she sent another frantic prayer that she hadn't inevitably invited one of those tantrums with her foolish Christmas wish.

By the time she reached the small, dank office Martin and a few of the senior crew used, she was willing her hands not to shake or her mind not to create wild scenarios. She took a fortifying sip of her coffee after Martin left, then almost jumped out of her skin as the phone trilled.

Calm down.

Taking a deep breath, she answered. 'Hello?'

'Gids, is that you?' the lazy voice, gone sultry over the years from fits of smoking to sound uncannily like their mother's, answered. Giada grimaced at the much-hated nickname Gigi had taken to calling her lately. There was no point asking her to stop. Her sister, like their mother, did what she wanted when she wanted.

'Yes, it's me.' She clutched the phone tighter. 'Is everything okay?'

'Well,' came the sighed response. 'I'm dying to say yes, sis, but I'm kinda in a spot of bother.'

'Kinda? Either you are or you aren't. Which is it?'

she demanded, her voice an octave higher and sharper than she'd intended.

'Goodness, Gids, I knew you'd hit DEFCON Five before I said two words.'

Giada could hear the eye roll in her sister's response. 'Gigi, we haven't spoken for weeks, and you've never called me while I've been away. I think it's fair to presume this isn't a welfare call. Whatever it is, just spit it out.' She squeezed her eyes shut for another fortifying moment before she blurted, 'Is it Mum?'

Her sister snorted. 'Way to lay the guilt trip, sis. And no, it's not Mum. Last I heard, she was in Rio getting a custom-fit costume done for Carnivale in February.'

'Please tell me she's not planning on staying there for Christmas? Or expecting us to join her?'

'Who knows? Though I think Christmas in Rio might be fun. I haven't been in ages.'

'Gigi.' Exasperation bled through her voice as she imagined a hellish two weeks with her mother and whatever menagerie of friends she'd picked up between London and Rio. She shook her head and zeroed in on what she could control. Like why her sister had called. 'What did you want to talk to me about?'

'Hold on,' Gigi yelled.

Giada gritted her teeth as raucous laughter and clinking glasses echoed down the phone. Then it quieted, indicating her sister had moved to a quieter area. Which disturbed Giada even further. Gigi didn't usually put much stock on discretion. 'Okay, first promise me this will stay between us?'

'What will?'

'Promise me first, then I'll tell you,' Gigi demanded.

'I've never betrayed your confidence.'

Unlike you.

She didn't add that, mostly because her twin didn't see anything wrong with blurting Giada's business to their mother, and also because her anxiety levels were climbing at an alarming rate already. She didn't need further angst.

'Yeah. Okay, fine. I may have taken possession of something that didn't quite belong to me.'

Giada inhaled sharply. 'Excuse me?' Her sister was many things, but she wasn't a thief. Until now apparently.

'Don't jump on your judgey horse so fast, Gids. There was a reason for it.'

Giada pulled off her woolly hat, suddenly feeling warm despite the cold dread coursing through her. 'What did you take? And what do you mean *was*?'

Her sister remained silent for several uncomfortable seconds during which Giada's vow to stay calm frayed badly.

'I took something important from this guy I was hoping to work for. Something that means a lot to him. And he's a very powerful guy.'

'Why?'

Gigi sniffed. 'Because he deserved it,' she spat without remorse.

At times like these, Giada wondered how they could be identical when their characters were night from day more often than not. 'Gigi—'

'Look, I was a little drunk when it happened, okay? And also, people shouldn't make promises they don't intend to keep.' Giada barely stopped herself from laughing hysterically, then offering the pot and kettle example because how many times had Gigi airily made a promise then promptly broken it? She was glad she didn't laugh, or she would've missed her sister's less heated, 'Especially men.'

Thoughts of laughter evaporated. 'Did he hurt you?' The memory of their mother's boyfriend who had ingratiated himself into their lives when they were fifteen and earned their trust only to emotionally abuse them was an unwanted but vivid memory. It was also one of the few times Giada and her sister had bonded in their pain.

If Giada were being meticulous, it was probably that incident that had triggered Gigi's dissonance with emotional responsibility. Deep down, Giada couldn't blame her. But it still hurt that *she'd* been swept up with the masses. 'Gigi, what did he do?' she prompted when her sister remained ominously silent.

'I met him a few months back and we sort of moved in the same circles for a while. I helped him to get info from someone I knew and he said I could work for him. Then he humiliated me publicly, claimed I was flighty and didn't have what it takes to be one of his precious team.'

Giada exhaled, her tension easing a touch. 'So this is about a job? Nothing else?'

An affronted huff echoed down the line. 'It's not just a job, Gids! Do you know the kinds of doors it will open for an influencer if I have Alessio Montaldi's endorsement?'

'No, I don't, since I don't have a clue who he is,' she

responded. 'And what exactly were you offering to do for him?'

'Whatever he asked. I would've done anything for him.'

Giada's eyes widened at her sister's low, husky and desperately voiced response. Another swell of dread washed over her. 'So he refused you the job. And you did what, exactly?'

Again, Gigi hesitated for heart-racing seconds. 'The thing I took…it was a family heirloom, Gids. And I…' She stopped and sucked in a breath and Giada took one right along with her, because she knew whatever was coming was big. And dreadful. 'He'd been looking for it for ever and had just found it the week before; was pretty obsessed with it actually. I think it played into some grand plan he was cooking up. Anyway, I thought he would take me seriously if I kept it for a while and then returned it.'

The creaking of plastic and the lance of pain through her fingers told Giada she was gripping the receiver too hard. 'When did you take it, Gigi?'

'Three weeks ago. I'd been trying for months to get him to change his mind about hiring me. I thought this would get his attention.'

'Look, just return his property and cut your losses. I'm sure you can find another—'

'I can't,' she interjected.

'Of course you can. Just return the thing, and apologise—'

'I can't return something I no longer have!'

'What do you mean you no longer have it?'

'Because I lost it three days ago.'

Giada dug the heel of her palm into her eyes, the dread she'd tried to hold at bay unfurling through her. 'Oh, God, Gigi.'

'I need you to help me, Gids. Please.'

'What can I do? I'm half a continent away.'

'But you're heading home soon, aren't you?' Gigi asked.

'Yes. For Christmas. With you and Mum.'

'That's not for another few weeks. I need you to help me out now. If Alessio discovers I've lost his property, I don't know what will happen. He's powerful and ruthless, Giada, and his reputation for not suffering fools isn't a joke.'

The protectiveness that was never far beneath the surface made Giada snap, 'I don't care about some power-hungry Italian who clearly likes to throw his weight around. When I get back you and I will talk to him and explain what's happened.'

Her sister snorted. 'He's not Italian. He's Sicilian. He already thinks I'm some useless airhead. I don't want to prove him right, Gids,' her sister said with a clear pout in her voice.

Giada wanted to roll her eyes at that but the lingering irritation wouldn't let her. 'Which is why I think you should come clean. Tell him what you've done and then speak to the authorities about recovering it.'

She could almost see her sister's careless shrug. 'I guess you don't care about me that much or the possibility that he can destroy my career with a few phone calls—'

'Gigi…'

Her sister huffed again. 'Are you going to help me or not?'

No.

The word hovered on the tip of Giada's tongue, ready to be set free.

But she knew how much her sister cared about her career. Plus Giada hadn't heard that thread of alarm in her sister's voice for over a decade. Ever since that final confrontation with Tom that had made her mother stare at Giada with something very close to hate ever since.

The harsh words spoken that had burst the false family bubble their mother had clung to, ignoring the emotional devastation going on under her nose. Giada knew Renata had never forgiven her for shattering that illusion.

'What do you want me to do?' she asked her sister.

'I need you to buy me time to find the heirloom.'

The speed of Gigi's response suggested she'd given it a lot of thought. Which was either a good thing or a bad thing. 'Fine. Give me this guy's number and I'll—'

'No. Jeez, Gids, you think I'd be calling you if a simple phone call would've cut it?'

'Then—?'

'I need you to distract him by pretending to be me for a few days while I try to find his item,' Gigi blurted.

'*What?* No. Absolutely not! You can't compound taking and losing his property by tossing subterfuge on top of it!'

'So you're saying I should just show up empty-handed and confess and hope he doesn't destroy my career or press charges against me?'

For the first time in a long time, Giada heard real desperation in her sister's voice. 'Gigi...'

'I know I don't have a PhD like you or some hotshot CEO but I know I can be a great fixer.' Her laugh was alarmingly self-deprecating. 'Hell, I do it for free for my friends all the time. All I'm asking is your help in fixing my mistake, Gids. He won't know who you are because you, shockingly, have zero social media presence. Trust me, I checked. Plus, only like...two people know I have a twin. So...please?'

Giada shut her eyes as her sister's plea bit into that vulnerable spot in her heart. As dread feathered down her spine.

Because she knew what her response was going to be even before she'd taken her next breath.

'How hard is it to find a slip of a woman who likes to give Bacchus a run for his money in the drinking stakes? Have you checked the cocktail bars on the French Riviera?' Alessio growled into the phone, his temper nearing simmering point.

These days, he prided himself on remaining unruffled. He expressed *some* emotions, sure. But letting any particular one—anger, bitterness—gain precedence over another?

Never. Not anymore.

There was a time when he'd been a slave to his emotions. But he'd learned, over long and arduous years, that there was untold advantage in doing the opposite. That his enemies writhed in indecision, wariness and suspicion when he displayed zero emotion. Just the way he wanted them. Those three flaws without fail granted him a means to exploit the chink in their armour that led to their downfall.

It'd served him well.

Except now he couldn't locate calm to save his life. Especially since all he heard at the end of the phone was nervous silence. 'Speak!'

A throat cleared. 'Apologies, *signor.* We've kept an eye on her usual haunts and explored many more. We've come up with nothing. She hasn't posted anything on her social media in over a week and she didn't go back to her apartment after her night out five days ago. My men searched the apartment, but we came up empty for the item.'

'So what you're saying is she's sniffed you out and gone to ground?'

'It seems so,' his trusted employee admitted with much chagrin.

While Alessio was furious at the outcome, he experienced the tiniest sliver of admiration for Gigi Parker. Perhaps he shouldn't have dismissed the airhead socialite quite so quickly. The team of fixers he'd sent after her were top-notch. Not his absolute best—they were currently engaged in another important task of ferreting out the last of his family's enemies and ensuring the final traps were properly laid for the reckoning he intended to deliver.

After years of meticulous planning, the perfect timing had been set—his mother's favourite time of year.

But he realised he'd underestimated Gigi. The flighty woman who'd imagined she could cajole and seduce her way into a job with him had some depth after all. At their meeting three months ago, he'd used the short ash-blonde hair, bold make-up and skimpy, thigh-skimming dresses to prejudge her.

His ultimate opinion *had* been cemented during the woeful fifteen-minute interview he'd had the misfortune of enduring with her. Perhaps if he'd stretched it to the full hour...?

Alessio dismissed the thought. It didn't matter. Yes, he'd been busy chasing the last cog in the wheel of restoring his family's honour and had taken his eye off the ball. But she'd stolen from him on a frivolous whim because she didn't get what she wanted.

Even worse, the Cresta Montaldi, the item she'd petulantly helped herself to, was one he'd spent the better part of a decade trying to retrieve.

There was no coming back from that.

If only Massimo could've been trusted to do his part, Alessio wouldn't be juggling a dozen balls in the air. How was it that the only person he came within a whisker of trusting turned out to be his playboy brother who didn't care a jot about the vendetta that had driven Alessio all his life?

He gritted his teeth and was about to issue a new set of ultimatums when the other man spoke. 'We talked to one of her friends. He said that she had plans to go to Switzerland. To Gstaad specifically.'

Surprise jolted him, then suspicion surged high.

'She's headed here? That's a little too convenient for her to be heading two hours away from my current location, don't you think? Surely, she wouldn't be that foolish?' Unless it was deliberate.

Was she taunting him?

While it wasn't rife public knowledge, it also wasn't a

secret how much the ruby-encrusted family crest meant to him. With the astronomical sums he'd promised for the heirloom's retrieval, it'd been whispered about enough for its value to be known.

'We thought so too but…isn't it worth exploring? Maybe she's trying to make contact through your brother?'

Alessio frowned, casting his eyes upwards as if he had X-ray vision that could see through the ceiling into the bedroom where Massimo was currently sleeping off another hangover. Alessio had thrown in the towel at three a.m., but he knew Massimo had stayed up with his friends until sunrise, which meant, despite it approaching noon, his brother wouldn't surface for another hour or two.

Alessio had come to Switzerland to drag his brother back to Sicily, to a family Christmas neither of them relished but that had to be performed for the sake of vows made to their mother.

After being apart for so many years due to circumstances beyond their control, it was an unyielding stipulation that they spent holidays and birthdays together. They hadn't missed one event in the last seven years.

Massimo had been his usual stubborn self, however, and Alessio had allowed himself to be talked into a rare weekend doing nothing but skiing and drinking, with the proviso that, come Monday, Massimo would get off his backside, off this mountain and onboard the private helicopter waiting to transport them to the airport.

Returning to Sicily was imperative to show his enemies that change and retribution were coming. That reclaiming his family name and everything else they'd

MAYA BLAKE   21

cruelly ripped from the Montaldis was only a matter of time.

'You've been tracking her for three weeks. Has she had contact with Massimo?' he pressed.

'Not that we've noticed. But your brother is an easier man to track than you.'

Teeth gritted, Alessio accepted that unfortunate truth.

While his younger brother had memories of what had happened to them in the past, he'd efficiently blocked it out by delving neck deep into a playboy lifestyle that usually set Alessio's teeth on edge and caused the endless headaches. But Alessio had made a vow to his mother on her deathbed that he would protect his baby brother come what may.

Vows were sacred.

If Massimo was somehow involved in this, Alessio suspected Christmas would be even more strained.

And if Gigi Parker was aiming to gain leverage by using his brother…well, that was something else he hadn't seen coming with this woman. But at least, he mused as his blood rushed faster at the thought of putting this nuisance to bed and being reunited with his possession, he was in the right place at the right time.

He took a deep breath as he relished teaching the little thief a lesson. It would be his pre-Christmas present to himself while righting a wrong.

Win-win.

'Look into it and give me an update immediately. Don't let me down,' he tossed in the warning. Keeping his men on their toes reaped results.

'*Se, signor,*' came the quick response.

He hung up and turned away from the desk in the study of the luxury chalet he'd owned for years but barely used himself. Striding to the wide rectangular window, he stared at the stunning white-out landscape.

Much as he preferred the warmer climes of Sicily, he couldn't deny that Gris-Montana in winter was stunning. Before it'd caught his interest, the sleepy town had been gaining popularity, though at a slower pace than its more flashy neighbours of Gstaad and Montreux. He'd taken steps to keep its charm, and it was a little gem he hadn't minded using for the odd weekend.

But this wasn't the time to stand idly admiring his view.

He had more important things to do.

Like bringing those who'd shattered his family to heel.

For that to happen, he needed to retrieve his possession from the elusive Gigi Parker.

Preferably on this side of Christmas.

A mere three hours later, Alessio was having to put the former on hold in favour of the latter. His men had pulled out all the stops to get him the answers he desired.

Gigi Parker was indeed in Gstaad.

She hadn't bothered to hide her movements, another reason she would be no good to him as a fixer. Above all else, he valued discretion, unless a certain…flair was required.

Like publicly ousting a certain president in Cardosia not so long ago. When he'd helped his friend Severino Valente to eject the corrupt head of state, Alessio had partly done it to show his enemies how long his reach extended.

But that was a one-off.

Gigi Parker's kind of flamboyance he could live without. Perhaps he'd teach her a lesson that would make her change her ways in future.

Or not.

He didn't really care one way or the other. All he cared about was retrieving his property.

Snatching up the keys to the fastest car in the fleet Massimo intended to test-drive before no doubt offering one up as his preferred Christmas present, Alessio stepped into the wide hallway of the sprawling chalet.

Massimo was swaggering down the stairs in black jogging bottoms and nothing else. He raked back his overly long hair before frowning at Alessio's coat and the gloves he held.

'You're going out?' he griped. 'After badgering me to get out of bed?'

'I need to head into Gstaad to retrieve something. I'll be back shortly.'

Massimo rolled his eyes. 'Of course, business finds you in the middle of a nowhere ski village. Do you ever let up?'

'No.' The growled answer made his brother's face tighten. The petulance left his expression, his eyes growing solemn as they regarded each other. 'I will never let up until my promise to Matri is kept.'

After a moment, Massimo's gaze dropped. He gave a curt nod before veering in the direction of the kitchen, probably in search of a hair of the dog. 'See you later, then. I might meet some friends for a late lunch if you're not going to be around for a few hours?' he threw over his shoulder.

Alessio exhaled irritably. He couldn't keep his brother under lock and key. Massimo was a grown man of thirty, if a little directionless, but Alessio planned to have another *direction* talk with him over the holidays.

Until then...

'Ciao,' he said, then paused with his hand on the door handle. *'Frati?'*

Massimo looked over his shoulder. *'Se?'*

'I'm meeting Gigi Parker. Do you know who she is?'

Massimo frowned. 'No. Should I?'

Alessio prided himself on spotting liars at a dozen paces. His brother's confusion was genuine. 'No. *Arrivederci.'*

The custom Lamborghini consumed the miles between Gris-Montana and Gstaad and delivered him to his destination in a little under two hours. By then the latest update had arrived. Despite it being only mid-afternoon, his team reported Gigi was in a well-known ski-resort bar. Touted as being exclusive, it'd long lost its right to exclusivity, Alessio knew, when financial constrictions had forced it to open its doors to all sorts of characters.

Features twisting with distaste, he tossed his keys to the valet and strode into the dark interior. Eyes tracked him and whispers followed soon after as he headed for the so-called VIP lounge. If nothing else, the owner of the establishment would get increased traffic over the holidays when it was announced Alessio Montaldi had dropped in.

Buon Natale at te.

Sneering at the sardonic thought, he stepped into the lounge.

In one corner, a raucous group high on their post-ski celebrations were downing shots as if a drought were imminent. Pockets of revellers gathered around fat armchairs while scantily clad waitresses darted back and forth, frantically serving clientele who were determined to outdrink each other.

The group that caught and held Alessio's attention, though, was the large one in the middle.

Specifically, the woman holding aloft a champagne bottle as if she were Lady Liberty herself while the other hand was propped on her curvy hip.

A craftily placed spotlight shone on her long ash-blonde hair, highlighting the thick, wavy strands that normally fell halfway down her back. With her head raised to the ceiling, however, the tapered tips caressed the top of her ass, drawing Alessio's attention to the rounded globes moulded by her silver sequinned dress.

The dress itself ended just below the tops of her thighs in a band of wispy feathers that swayed when she rolled her hips in time to the sultry music.

At her next risqué pose, the group cheered then started chanting her name. 'Gigi! Gigi! Gigi!'

She rolled her hips faster, the motion hypnotic, as she fell under the spell of the music and her adoring fans.

Slowly, her body pivoted his way, presenting him with her profile.

Alessio frowned as heat swelled in his middle, then flowed up his chest to his throat. His hands clenched within his coat pockets, his shoulders tensing for reasons he couldn't fathom.

Had the Gigi he met months ago gained curves since their last meeting? Were her lips a little fuller, too?

And the look she was casting the males in her group seemed almost…coquettish, whereas she'd been brazen with Alessio.

Had he also missed the fact that Gigi Parker possessed impressive chameleon-like tendencies? His nostrils flared with irritation. Because again, what did it matter? Their final interaction wouldn't extend beyond tonight. Once he retrieved his property and delivered his lesson.

Which he couldn't do from across the room.

So why couldn't he move?

Why was his gaze rapt on the woman putting on a tasteless show for half a dozen men and women who seemed equally enthralled? And why did their slavish attention send a pulse of fury through him?

'Sir, can I get you—?'

Alessio dismissed the waitress with a curt head shake, his total focus on the woman now crooking her finger towards one man in the group. The guy fell out of his chair onto his knees, then eagerly crawled to deliver himself at her feet.

The slim arm holding the champagne slowly lowered and tipped towards the young man, who happily opened his mouth to receive the fizzing liquid. More laughter broke out as Gigi anointed him with her drink, drenching him in the process to his utter delight.

When she paused, he surged forward eagerly, bracing his hands on her hips.

Alessio's feet moved, fury inexplicably mounting.

He told himself it was because he'd had enough of

this spectacle. But as he approached them, the urge to remove those hands from her hips grew into unreasonable proportions, until he could feel a growl bubbling in his throat.

'Who. Is. Next?' The object of his focus cocked her hips sharply as she shouted the question, effectively dislodging the hands on her hips and lowering Alessio's temperature.

'No one. Because your little party is over.'

Shouts of outrage erupted and died just as quickly when heads swivelled his way and expressions morphed from surprise to shock to wariness as whispers travelled through the crowd.

In the centre, Gigi froze, her smoky-grey, almond-shaped eyes widening before her mouth fell open.

He had to give her credit for her acting skills.

The rapid rise and fall of her chest and the light quiver that seemed to go through her, making the magnum of champagne slip from her wet grasp to thump, forgotten, on the cheap carpet, was a good touch.

The fast blink as her gaze left his face and did a quick scrutiny of his body before she sucked in a shaky breath? An ace performance that would've fooled a slow-witted man.

But he'd been subjected to far too many forms of deceit for it to work with him. And despite the curious heat unfurling through him, he tightened his jaw, one eyebrow elevated as he waited for her next move.

Her eyelids descended for a moment before she raised them to meet his gaze again.

'Mr Montaldi... Alessio, what a lovely surprise!'

CHAPTER TWO

GIADA WILLED HER heart to stop attempting to escape her ribcage.

Her nerves were already eating her alive. The last thing she wanted was to worsen her predicament by collapsing in a heap. For starters, it would put a swift end to her ruse and blow her cover wide open.

Plus, she suspected the black carpet beneath her feet held substances she wouldn't like her skin to come into contact with.

But try as she might, she couldn't stop her racing pulse. Because it was registering far too late that clicking through hundreds of internet images of this man from the safety of her London bedsit was one thing. Being confronted with the flesh-and-blood version, the mile-wide-shouldered and towering-several-inches-over-six-foot version, was a whole different ball of yarn.

Not to mention those eyes.

In the dark interior of the club, she couldn't tell whether they were dark gold, bronze or hazel. But she knew how effectively they could reduce mere mortals to stupefied messes because they were scrambling her brain cells *right now*.

She'd been deeply sceptical when Gigi had insisted she only needed to install herself at L'Illusion in time for the *apres-ski* crowd to draw the attention of Alessio Montaldi's team of fixers.

Truth be told, Giada had tried not to think too deeply about how invasive Alessio would have to be to locate anyone at his whim. Then she'd hoped he'd send his minions to buy herself some time before she met the man himself. Because even two weeks after that phone call with Gigi and agreeing to this mad ploy, Giada had known she wasn't ready.

Exhibit one—the way she'd greeted him just now.

She'd forgotten to ask Gigi how to address the imposing, dynamic man looking down at her with hooded eyes, disdain dripping from every bronzed, polished pore.

With every bone in her body, she yearned to turn away from his judgemental stare, brace her hands on her knees and suck in the much-needed oxygen he'd seemingly depleted from the room with his presence.

But she'd promised her sister she would do whatever it took to buy time for Gigi to rectify her mistake. She couldn't let her down at the first hurdle.

Before she could speak, though, Jean-Luc finally rose from his submissive position on the carpet, his arm creeping around her waist as he smiled down at her.

'Everything okay, *chérie*?' he slurred, totally oblivious to the fact that his champagne-drenched shirt was sticking to her bare arm. Or that he'd drawn the merciless attention of their visitor.

Giada shimmied away from him with a light laugh she didn't feel. 'Of course!'

She'd noticed very quickly that Jean-Luc was the handsy type, prone to caressing a wrist, arm or hip in the name of tipsy friendliness, and had been inventing creative ways of combating a situation Gigi would've laughingly indulged.

Her heart jumped into her throat when Alessio's eyes shifted back to her and narrowed.

Had she given herself away already?

Swallowing, she went for broke. Striding forward on precariously spindly high heels, she rested her hands on his arms, raised herself on tiptoe and brushed a kiss across Alessio Montaldi's cheek.

Dear God...he smelled amazing. Like the ocean blended with wood smoke.

She trapped a stunned moan before it escaped, just as the thick arms beneath her fingers went rigid, then flexed, right before his body froze.

Was it her imagination or did he suck in a sharp breath?

When the heat pulsing off his body threatened to scramble her brain further, she hurriedly cleared her throat. 'I didn't know you were in town.'

His jaw rippled, his gaze fixated on her when she took a vital step back. 'Did you not?'

The sound of his voice, a deep, low rumble of oiled gravel, quaked right through her, leaving tiny explosions she barely stopped from gasping out loud.

Snatching in a breath, she widened her smile. 'Of course not. I would've made sure we connected for a drink. For old times' sake, if nothing else.'

He stared at her for several terrifying seconds before he exhaled. 'I'd advise you not to play games with me, Miss Parker.'

When the group inhaled a collective breath, Alessio slowly turned his head to survey the band of merry acquaintances she'd fallen into forty-eight hours ago. Giada wasn't sure whether to be glad or insulted on their behalf that he'd already forgotten about them.

'I will pay your tab for the rest of the night if you leave us,' he offered silkily, his tone totally belying the tempered rage vibrating off his body.

The ragtag group stared slack-jawed at him. Then excited whispers broke out.

When Jean-Luc attempted to reach for her again, his fingers inches from her bare shoulder, Alessio speared him with laser-sharp eyes. 'Now.' The directive was soft and deadly.

A split second later, with a chorus of *'au revoir'* and air-kisses, they rushed to the bar, eagerly shouting their orders at the bartender.

Alone with Alessio Montaldi and his laser gaze, Giada could barely breathe. Tension mixed with panic churned her insides as she forced another smile. 'Oops. Looks like you've scared my friends away. What am I going to do with myself for the rest of the evening?'

He took a step closer, forcing her to tilt her head to meet his gaze. His hands remained in his pockets but his gaze roved freely over her face, neck, down her throat to the risqué dip in her dress that exposed far too much cleavage.

When it rose again, the disdain had thickened, but something else lurked within the dark depths. Something she couldn't name but which sent a lance of dangerous heat through her.

'Here's a suggestion. With one phone call, I could have you arrested. Would you prefer that?'

Wild panic seized her before she breathed through it. With a move worthy of an academy award, she dragged her fingers through her hair in the slow, languid way she'd seen Gigi perform a thousand times. Breath held, she watched him track that motion too, a peculiar flame leaping in his eyes. Could she get away with licking her lips now? Or would it be too over the top?

Giada didn't want to decode why heat unfurled in her pelvis at the thought. Instead, she settled for tilting her head to one side and delivering a slow, heated smile, hoping it didn't betray the nervous yet weirdly powerful sensation flowing through her. 'Of course, I wouldn't prefer that. But you don't need to prove you're the big and powerful Alessio Montaldi. I know I'm completely at your mercy.' She dropped her gaze to examine her scarlet-tipped nails. 'Or am I?' she taunted softly, the way she'd seen Gigi tease men far too often.

Pivoting away from him without waiting for his response—mostly to hide her nerves—she sashayed over to the low sofa that backed against the wall of the lounge, supremely conscious of every inch of her body.

Lowering herself into it, she made a show of crossing her legs while she watched him from beneath her lashes.

His eyes narrowed to slits and his jaw turned to stone as he prowled forward. Fully expecting him to take the seat next to her, she was stunned when he perched on the coffee table directly in front of her.

With his hands out of his pockets, elbows braced

on his knees and his body angled forward, he'd effectively blocked her gaze of the lounge, making himself the total focus of her attention. 'I caution you against toying with me, Miss Parker.'

She flipped her hair again. 'It's Gigi. I'm sure I've told you to call me that before?'

'You have. And do you remember my response when you did?' he batted back, his incisive gaze giving her nowhere to hide.

Oh, no.

Giada lowered her lashes. She couldn't keep staring into those piercing eyes and not give herself away.

What had Gigi advised?

'Keep the conversation general. He has a mind like a steel trap. He'll eat you alive on the specifics.'

She waved a carefree hand then dropped it onto her thigh. When his gaze followed, she fought the urge to fidget. 'Probably something formal and stuffy. But as you can tell, I'm not one for following rules.'

'Believe me, that hasn't escaped me. Where is my property?' he snapped.

She jumped, then forced another laugh. 'Straight to business, I see. Not even going to buy me a drink first?'

'No. And you and I have no business together. You stole something that belongs to me. You're a fool if you think you have any leverage at all in this situation.'

A flash of fury lit her veins. 'I don't like being called names, Alessio.' Especially that one. Her mother had called her foolish far too many times for every action Giada had taken that wasn't rubber-stamped by Renata DiMarco. Like Giada wanting to further her education. Or refusing to endorse her mother's extravagant spending sprees to Paris with money they couldn't afford. 'In fact, being insulted makes me very disagreeable.'

'You don't?' he taunted. 'That's surprising since you're actively collecting them with your every action. Another one that springs to mind is thief,' he tossed in cruelly.

Giada knew she—or rather her sister—deserved that one. But still her ire rose. 'If I took your property, and I'm not admitting to anything, did you stop to think it was to prove a point? That I might even be helping you?' she challenged.

Gigi's actions had been misguided and unfortunate, and her insistence that Alessio would *eventually* appreciate the reason had sounded sceptical to Giada. Only pure desperation made her toss it at him now.

From the furious incredulity on his face, he thought so too. 'No, because whatever point you were hoping to make lost relevancy when you resorted to stealing.'

It chafed that he had a point there too. In innumerable ways, what Gigi had done was wrong. But after meeting Alessio Montaldi, Giada could guess what had driven her sister to such rash action.

The man was fascinating. And unnerving. Infuriating and wholly possessing of a dynamism so hypnotising, she could see how everyone cowered and fell silent when he spoke. How, even now, the waitresses gave him a wide berth and the crowd watched him furtively, on the edge of their seats as if awaiting some marvellous exhibition they could later recount with bated breath.

She couldn't blame them.

She was on the mental edge of her seat. Toss in that sense-scrambling scent of ocean-cum-smoked wood aftershave pulsing from his skin, and the effect of those dark burnished eyes, and she feared she would soon be on the *literal* edge of her seat.

Unless she pulled herself together. Now.

'Even if the alleged act was exposing the flaws in your security? Perhaps you left yourself wide open and someone getting their hands on your property...hypothetically...may or may not have been a piece of cake.'

His jaw turned to granite. 'You have exactly one minute to tell me where my property is or—'

'I think we've established by now that I don't rise to threats, Alessio,' she interrupted, twirling a strand of hair around her finger even as her heart beat wildly like a trapped bird. 'So whatever you're planning on terrifying me with next, I'll probably just...you know... *scoff* at.'

His nostrils flared. His eyes darkened. Whether it was out of fury or because hearing his name might have triggered the same reaction it did in her, she wasn't willing to explore.

'During our last meeting, you struck me as many things, Miss Parker, but extremely reckless didn't strike me as one of them.'

Her heart stuttered at his arctic tone.

Giada should probably have dialled down the taunts then. The furious man before her was clearly running out of patience. But for the life of her, she couldn't back down.

It felt weirdly *invigorating* that she'd managed to needle him. Twirling another strand of hair, she smiled. 'Call it a new skill if you want.'

His head twitched back. Only by a tiny fraction but

she could see the sliver of bewilderment in his eyes. As if he could barely believe her audacity.

Giada was marvelling at her gumption when he surged to his feet.

For an age he stared down at her. Every atom of her body was infused with so much electricity, Giada believed she would spontaneously combust.

His gaze slowly raked over her. Once. Twice.

Heat dragged up from her toes and she knew her lips were parted, her breasts straining against the already tight material of her dress. When her tongue dashed out to ease the tingle in her bottom lip, she allowed it.

She told herself it was okay to react this way because her sister had never been shy of embracing her sexuality. Gigi would never feel uncomfortable under such blatant male scrutiny. She would revel in it and give as good as she got.

But while Giada would withstand such a bold, unapologetic stare, she couldn't bring herself to return the favour. Not when the man in question was so...*potent.* So overwhelmingly untamed and *sexy.*

As much as Giada didn't want to admit it, Alessio Montaldi was an exemplary male specimen. The kind she wasn't in the habit of fraternising with...ever. The men she usually encountered were scientists who lived and breathed their jobs or benign betas who were friendly enough and nowhere near intimidating.

Alessio Montaldi *breathed* superior alpha male. He was the king of all he surveyed and with every bone in his body he owned it.

But he doesn't own you.

The tiny little but empowering thought raised her

chin, sparks of defiance igniting through her as he stared at her.

That defiance took a steep nosedive, however, when in the next moment he bent low and scooped her up.

She yelped as dizziness rushed her and her world turned literally upside down. Before Giada could fathom what was happening, Alessio was striding through the throng of clubbers.

Dear God, he'd tossed her over his shoulder!

'What the hell do you think—?'

'If you know what's good for you, you'll stop talking right now,' he growled.

Giada opened her mouth to rip a volley of words at him, but her throat dried up when warm hands landed at the backs of her thighs, sending sizzling showers of heat all through her body.

She knew it was only to keep her from tumbling over his shoulder, but the moan that escaped unbidden from her throat was luckily drowned out by the music and chatter that greeted the spectacle she no doubt made being carried out like a sack of potatoes.

Heat that had nothing to do with her inverted position, and everything to do with her way her breasts were pressed into his back, rushed into her face. The way his muscles rippled beneath her hands when she had no choice but to grab his coat to steady herself pushed her to ignore his warning. 'Put me down right now!'

'Are you sure? You seem to enjoy making a spectacle of yourself. I'm only obliging you,' he drawled, his voice still that infuriatingly steady rumble that burrowed into places she didn't want to name.

Giada sucked in a breath when he took the stairs

that led outside in quick strides, uncaring that he was jostling her against his body. When she reached out to steady herself once more, her hands grabbed the firm hard globes of his ass.

He stiffened, then stopped.

Giada squeezed her eyes shut as mortification erupted through her.

She opened her mouth to say something, *anything* to abate the charged atmosphere she'd created. But Alessio was snapping something at the nightclub staff, who were hurrying to respond.

Then he was striding out of the entrance.

His threats weren't working.

Alessio couldn't recall the last time he'd been so thoroughly stumped.

He would've been inclined to believe Gigi Parker was off her head with drink or perhaps even drugs, had he not looked into her eyes. Stunning eyes that sparked with equal parts defiance and intelligence. Eyes that dared him to do his worst while holding a touch of nervous...anticipation?

Hand her over to the authorities. Let them deal with it.

He knew several high-positioned individuals in law enforcement across two dozen countries, including this one. He could have her in handcuffs within the next fifteen minutes.

So why was he hesitating?

And why the hell was he unable to take his eyes... or hands...off her?

She'd barely registered on his radar in the two weeks

he'd spent in Europe during the summer when he'd been fixing a few problems for several members of royal families who'd repeatedly got themselves ensnared in scandals.

She'd been on the fringes of a particularly hard-partying bunch of socialites and trustfundistas who'd consistently ended up in the tabloids. Alessio had only taken note of her because her passable PR skills had come in handy when his team had needed it.

He wasn't entirely sure why he'd agreed to her request for an interview. Perhaps he'd had one too many whiskies? Or he'd been frustrated that his efforts to locate the Cresta Montaldi had repeatedly failed?

Whatever the case, he'd seemingly created a monster by obliging her.

But had his monster been *this* beguiling?

What did it matter? Acting like a caveman wasn't his preferred behaviour. But he couldn't allow her to continue to twirl her hair and bat her eyelashes at him as if he were some simple hormonal teenager eager for attention from a beautiful woman. His phone contacts were filled with women ready to share his bed at the crook of his finger.

So why are you so affected *by her*?

Because she was in possession of the very thing his father had died for.

The object his mother had despaired would never be regained and returned to their family in time to restore their reputation before she died. She'd faded away without that hope ever being realised. It stuck in his craw that this slip of a woman could be so cavalier with something so profoundly fundamental to who he was.

To *what* he was—the firstborn of a once-respected Sicilian family going back generations. A family he was determined to make whole again.

So *se*, he planned on delivering a few lessons before he was done with her.

And if that meant suffering through his brain latching onto how smooth her skin was, how her curves sank into his body, how lush her ass seemed from the corner of his eye? *Bene*, suffer he would.

'Put me down right now,' she shouted.

Jaw gritting against the insufferable heat surging through his veins and pooling in his groin, he stepped out of the club, strode to where the valet had fastidiously parked his vehicle, and lowered her unceremoniously to the ground next to his passenger door.

Alessio then watched her blink rapidly and scramble to push back her long silky hair, refusing to imagine if this was the way she looked when she was thoroughly made love to in bed. He almost welcomed the spiky glare she sent his way. The fact it only raised his temperature created a rumble in his chest he barely managed to stifle before it ripped free.

'Where's my coat? It's freezing out here.'

He wanted to snap that she should've thought of that before defying him, but he suspected it would only instigate more stubborn rebellion.

Instead, he found himself shrugging out of his own coat, stepping close to tuck it around her shoulders before gathering the lapels closer.

For a frozen moment, he thought he caught stunned surprise in her eyes at his gesture, before the entitled pout made a return, her glare turning fiercer as he reached for the door to his sports car.

'I'm not leaving without my—'

The words died in her throat as, per his instructions, the bouncer approached with her belongings. When she immediately went to shrug off his coat, he stepped back, a firm reluctance to have her take it off tunnelling through him.

'Keep it. The sooner we get out of here, the safer you'll be from my urge to throttle you.'

Again, he caught a flash of surprise at his heated words.

Se, he was mildly astounded himself. Was he a red-blooded Sicilian prone to vividly imagining how he would take down his enemies? *Certo.* Was he prone to blurting out those urges as if he were starring in a mindless reality TV show? Absolutely not.

'Get in,' he clipped out, yanking the door open the moment she'd snatched her purse and a wholly inappropriate sparkly coat from the bouncer—without a word of thanks, he noted.

She opened her mouth, no doubt to throw another taunt his way.

Alessio hardened his features, letting her see how close she was to breaking his last straw.

Luminous smoky-grey eyes blinked again.

She glanced inside the car. Her throat started to move in a nervous swallow, but she halted the move at the last moment. He'd seen it though, and satisfaction pulsed through him.

Good, she wasn't utterly devoid of a sense of self-preservation.

But when she glanced at the door to the nightclub, he stepped into her eyeline. 'You're not going back in there. At least not tonight. Accept that and get in the car. This game you're playing ends tonight.'

The faintest fluttering of her nostrils, and she shrugged off all concern.

For a fraction of a moment, Alessio envied her easy ability to bat off responsibility and burdens. It'd never been a luxury he could indulge in. Not since his childhood was mercilessly ripped from him.

He smothered that bite of envy when she responded. 'You're right. Let's do this. The quicker we both get what we want, the quicker I can get back to my friends, right?'

His nostrils flared as she angled her body with exaggerated grace that nevertheless consumed all his attention, his compelled gaze falling to the long, exposed legs she lifted off the ground to slide into the footwell. *Dulce cielo.*

He shut the door with suppressed emotion and rounded the car.

Sliding behind the wheel, he willed his senses to calm. Willed the tingling and fury and bewilderment to cease.

He had duties to perform. Wrongs to right. And this woman…sexy and infuriating—*why was her scent so intoxicating?*—wasn't going to stand in his way.

Alessio glanced at the clock. Time he didn't have was ticking away. 'You have thirty seconds to decide where we go once I start the car. I suggest the destination be wherever you're hiding my property. And don't say your hotel room to buy yourself more time. I have it on good authority it isn't there. But be warned, if you don't tell the truth…if you let me decide what happens next, you won't like the consequences.'

CHAPTER THREE

GIADA PRETENDED TO look out of the window at the neon sign of the nightclub to buy herself thinking time. To swallow the trepidation thickening in her throat.

According to Gigi, Alessio was a cold, unfeeling shark. An entitled alpha male with a rock for a heart who ruthlessly shredded opponents in his wake.

Well, his actions in the last ten minutes indicated otherwise. Even now, emotion pulsed from him, his fingers clamped around the steering wheel, chest rising and falling as he speared her with volcanic eyes. She still hadn't quite worked out their colour but they burned holes into her skin.

With every moment that passed, though, she grew more impressed with his rigid control. Just as she'd been awed by the hard, packed muscled beneath his—

No.

She was absolutely not going to think about his body. About that granite-hard jaw, those chiselled cheekbones and the way their perfect angles crafted his breathtaking face. About the sensual mouth that hinted strongly at his Latin blood and barely restrained passions—

Enough.

She shook her head to dispel the sensual web weaving dangerously around her. Giada wasn't sure why he affected her so strongly, but she wouldn't allow this insanity to continue.

Think, think. What had he said again?

Right. More threats about jail or worse.

She took a deep breath, almost groaning in despair when, from the corner of her eye, she saw his fingers tighten harder around the wheel.

No, he most certainly wasn't unfeeling when it came to his possession.

Scrambling to recall everything Gigi had said, she cleared her throat and faced him. 'I'll return your item. Before that, though, you owe me.'

Cold incredulity flashed in his eyes. *'Sei serio adesso?'* *Are you serious right now?*

'Sì, io sono.' Giada wasn't sure why she answered in her mother's language. Why uttering the husky words sent a pulse of…*something* through her veins. Or even why Alessio inhaled sharply, as if the same *something* spiralling through her afflicted him too.

All she knew was that she had to take proper control or, *dear God*, she risked losing her mind and scuppering this mission before she was of any use to her sister.

Fingers gripping the rich woollen coat doing a sterling job of warming her body, she ploughed ahead. 'I'm only asking for what you failed to deliver during our last meeting. For starters, you cut the interview short. You said some pretty unpleasant things and you prejudged me without giving me a chance to defend myself. I think that was wrong and unfair. If nothing else, you owe me for helping you with the situation in Monaco.'

Giada secretly exhaled in relief for delivering it with confidence. Somehow, she'd suspected it might come in handy.

She'd made Gigi repeat this part over and over so she didn't get it wrong, all while being secretly appalled her sister wanted to work for this man in spite of the awful way he'd treated her.

That confidence threatened to dissolve when Alessio narrowed his eyes. 'You're serious,' he mused harshly, in English this time. 'You want me to interview you right now? After your actions, I'd be a fool to let you anywhere near my business.'

Giada forced a shrug, even as apprehension at delving deeper into this subterfuge ate like acid through her bones. 'Or you'll get the chance to see my full potential. After all, if I can swipe your precious family crest right from under your nose...'

His jaw gritted at the reminder. 'What you're forgetting is that I employ fixers, not con-women or cat burglars. And most definitely not petty thieves.'

'And I'm none of those things. I told you, it was a spur-of-the-moment thing to prove a point. Oh, and I don't just want an interview,' she tagged on bravely.

'*Santi copra,*' he cursed under his breath.

She rushed on before the volcanic rumble became a full explosion. 'Your reputation as a hard taskmaster is well known. But so is the fact that you can be even-handed when it suits you.'

His gaze threatened to flay her. 'You think pandering to my vanity will swing things your way?'

In truth, she'd hoped it would.

Men in his position tended to love shameless sycophants. But clearly this man was cut from a different cloth. 'No. I suspect you believe you have the biggest balls when you walk into any room whether anyone cares or not. But I *am* hoping you have the integrity to go with that ego. So this is my ask—set me a task. Let me fix something for you. If I fail, you get your crest back and we go our separate ways, no harm no foul.'

'And if you pass?' His tone held decisive scorn, his belief that she would fail throbbing through every syllable.

Giada's fingers tightened around his coat to hide their shaking, praying she wasn't digging a deeper hole for her sister by heading down this perilous path. Giada didn't have the first clue how to be a fixer for a molten-eyed Sicilian who looked set to emulate the emblematic volcano that soared its majesty in his homeland. 'You give me a role on your team or write a good enough reference for me to land a similar job elsewhere.'

Silence, thick and charged, reigned in the car for a full minute.

Giada urged herself not to fidget.

When it got too much, she flicked her gaze up from where she'd pinned it on the dashboard. As suspected, his gleaming eyes were fixed on her, his expression inscrutable. Calculating. She didn't dare be relieved he was no longer furious, not when he was examining her like a specimen under a powerful microscope.

'You want a job with me this badly?' he drawled, his accent a little more pronounced, drawing further tingles over her body.

Saying yes felt like admitting to much, *much* more.

But she'd boxed herself into this corner. She had no choice but to respond. 'Yes, I do.'

'Where was this fire back in Monaco? Back then, you were more interested in the perks of the job, not the job itself, if memory serves.'

Giada silently berated her sister for her flakiness. Then shrugged again. 'That was then, this is now. Do we have a deal?'

She hadn't seen it happen, but Alessio's fingers were no longer clenched around the wheel. Somehow one wrist rested on top of it now, and he'd angled his body and draped his other arm over the back of her seat. In the semi-dark interior of the car, his large body reclined like a lazy predator sizing up its prey.

The knots in her belly tightened as awaited his answer. She had zero recourse if he decided he'd had enough and handed her over to the authorities. Her only hope was that he wanted the quickest path to retrieving his property and wouldn't want to bother with the bureaucratic red tape of dealing with the police.

Or, as a fixer, he might want to do things his own way...

Caution whispered through her, diverting her focus from his far too fascinating face to the door.

From the corner of her eye, she caught his hard smirk. 'Rethinking your own ultimatums, Miss Parker?' Silky, dangerous words that feathered alarmed tingles over her body.

Giada tried to hide her shivery reaction by boldly meeting his gaze, chin raised. 'Not at all. I'm only wondering how long you intend to keep me in dramatic suspense.'

A ripple went through his jaw but before he could respond, an incoming text beeped loudly.

Panic rolled through Giada as she frantically tried to recall if her phone was still off.

They'd agreed on radio silence until Gigi found the heirloom, lest it tipped Alessio off, but Gigi marched to the beat of her own drum.

Relief coursed through her when Alessio fished his phone from his breast pocket. Irritation flashed across his face as he glanced at the text, his face clenching even tighter at whatever he read. Then she watched his fingers fly over the screen for a minute in a series of quick-fire responses before he thrust the phone away.

He exhaled, then pinned her with his laser gaze. 'You have your deal, Miss Parker.' Before she could accommodate the tiniest sliver of triumph, he was continuing, 'But it will be conducted on my terms.'

With a flick of his strong fingers, the powerful engine roared to life.

Like a candle exposed to a gust of air, her relief snuffed out. 'What's that supposed to mean? What terms?'

He didn't answer immediately.

Instead, he leaned forward, making her shrink back in her seat as he reached for her seat belt. He saw her reaction, a thin, cruel smile curving his lips, content to keep her in alarmed suspense as he secured her belt, then dealt with his own.

Then with the adeptness of a man in supreme control, he shot the car into traffic.

It wasn't until he'd pulled up at the first traffic sign that he answered. 'I've wasted enough time chasing after you. From now until this farce is over and you accept that you don't have what it takes to make it on any of my teams, I own your time. And you,' he finished in a silken voice fat with satisfaction. 'But a word of caution. Attempt anything underhanded and you'll learn the true meaning of consequences. *Capisci?*'

She'd got what she wanted and bought Gigi the precious time she needed. So why were alarm bells tolling louder in her ears? Giada tried subtly shaking her head to dispel the klaxon, but it only grew louder.

'I said, am I understood?' he pressed, that false indolence making him all the more terrifying.

Giada realised then that the tolling wasn't just in her head. The lights had turned green and horns were blaring behind them. Alessio ignored the irate drivers, his gaze fixed on her as he awaited her response.

'Yes. I understand,' she blurted, then gulped down her apprehension as satisfaction spread on his face.

His thigh muscles rippling beneath his trousers, he slid the car into gear and shot forward. Despite the glitz and glamour of Gstaad in winter, heads still turned as he cut through traffic.

Giada's thoughts continued to spin, alternating between being thankful she'd bought Gigi much-needed time, and fretting about what exactly she'd let herself in for.

Which was why it took depressingly long minutes to realise Alessio had driven to the cheap hotel she'd booked into. It didn't take as long to read the disdain on his face, however.

'You have ten minutes to pack your things,' he announced, his gaze flicking from the shady entrance to her face.

Her heart flung itself against her ribcage. 'Pack my… Why, where are we going?'

One silky eyebrow arched. 'Questioning me already?'

'I'm not following you blindly, if that's what you think,' she whipped back, more out of apprehension than anything else. Because that bell? It was clanging louder and this time it had nothing to do with irate drivers. 'And I suspect no one who works for you does either.'

Something glinted in his eyes, gone too quickly for her to decipher. 'I'm returning to Sicily in the morning. Tonight, we're spending the night at my chalet in Gris-Montana. Your interview will begin when we reach the chalet. You now have seven minutes, Miss Parker,' he warned with deadly softness.

Fevered questions tumbled on her tongue, but instinct warned her that Alessio would leap on any excuse to default her. For Gigi's sake, she couldn't hand him that excuse.

Aware of the seconds ticking away, Giada opened the door.

The two-star hotel located on a quiet side street with dim lighting and kitsch decor had seen better days, and, unlike the plush resorts and five-star hotels, the icy pavements hadn't been well swept or at all in some places.

Forgetting that she was wearing the sky-high heels her twin favoured and was way more adept at walking in, Giada stepped out, took a single step and immediately teetered wildly.

Dread and impending shame scrambled through her, a helpless cry breaking from her throat as the pavement rushed up at her.

At the last moment, and with dizzying speed that snatched her breath away, a thick, muscled arm swept her off her feet, as Alessio pulled her back against his hard torso.

Despite the layers separating them, his body heat suffused hers, his scent wrapping around her so entirely that Giada barely managed to bite back a moan it was so appealing.

Her limbs went weak and loose, her head spinning from the effects of the near accident and his hard embrace. She wasn't sure how long he held her, only that she could feel every twitch and play of his muscles. Feel the intense awareness of his manliness. Reminding her that she hadn't been held like this for a very long time.

Not since her last, brief relationship fizzled and died under the stress of long-distance apathy.

An engine backfired in the distance. Above them, a weak bulb flickered.

Giada shook her head, willing back a modicum of the perspective she seemed to lose around this man.

'I… You can let me go now. Thanks,' she tagged on hurriedly, then cringed when her voice emerged low and husky. Almost…*turned on*.

He didn't respond or heed her request. Seconds ticked away as he held her.

Giada pressed her lips together, a little reticent to speak again in case her breathlessness betrayed her.

Alessio walked forward, still holding her captive, until they reached the double doors that led to the dingy little hotel lobby. His breath washed over her cheek, her only sign that he was leaning in closer still. 'Five minutes,' he said, low and fierce in her ear.

The second he set her down, Giada pushed away, eager to be free from his intoxicating presence. Because for several seconds, all she'd wanted was to remain plastered against the pillar of masculine heat, to receive every ounce of warmth from him and not the coat she still held onto.

She didn't need to look back to know he was watching her like a hawk, probably even following her into the building. Deciding to shun the elevator and take the stairs since she was only on the first floor, she rushed away, the giddy pounding of her pulse making her question whether the course she was taking was a wise one.

Batting away the warning—because, really, what choice did she have?—she went down another dimly lit hallway and pressed her key card to the lock.

Since she'd been on tenterhooks and out of her depth to do more than grab what she needed when she needed it, she hadn't fully unpacked.

In under a minute, she was done.

She considered texting Gigi to let her know what was happening but decided against it. It was too risky—

Thoughts and body froze when she opened the door to see Alessio leaning against the wall opposite, his hands once again shoved into his pockets.

'You didn't need to follow me up.'

'Didn't I?' he rasped with a lifted eyebrow that mocked her question.

'What do you think I was going to do? Run away? After getting you to agree to what I want?' she scoffed.

For an instant, a vicious harshness flared in his eyes. Giada wasn't sure which part of her response had caused it but she was relieved when it disappeared just as quickly. 'As long as you're in possession of what belongs to me, you can be assured that I won't take my eyes off you.'

Why that sent a sizzling trail of fire down every inch of her spine was too unsettling to contemplate. Then he was robbing her of breath all over again by stepping forward abruptly and relieving her of the small suitcase.

Giada told herself he'd done it out of suspicion, not chivalry. The tension riding him as he headed for the stairs without looking back said so.

His clipped, 'It's been taken care of,' when she approached the reception desk to pay her bill and check out sent yet another spark of alarm through her.

The strange sensations continued to course through her as he stowed her case in the car and pointedly held the door open for her.

She found her voice a minute later, frowning at his stiff profile. 'I was perfectly capable of checking out for myself. You didn't need to do it.'

His mouth twisted, dragging her attention to its sensual curve. 'I didn't do it for you, *duci*. There's only so much of the stench I could breathe in from that filthy lobby before I caught something incurable.' He slanted her a glance, his voice dripping more of his seemingly customary disdain. 'I'm beginning to understand the gravity of your need for employment.'

Since Giada couldn't state the truth or confess that

she hadn't given the hotel much more than a cursory glance after ensuring it had a bed she could sleep in and was priced within her budget, she had to let his comment slide despite its harsh sting. Keeping her gaze on the road, she shrugged. 'How far are we going?'

She felt his sharp look on her face.

'Eager to get back to your friends?' His tone held a distinct note of displeasure, making her hesitate before issuing a resounding *yes*.

She was supposed to be eager for a job, after all.

'Not at all. You'll recall I mentioned I wasn't going to follow you blindly. As for my friends, they'll be here when you and I are done.'

If anything, the atmosphere grew more charged. A little bewildered, Giada glance at him. His gaze was fixed ahead, his hands curled around the steering wheel in an easy grip that didn't disguise his tension as they stopped at another red light.

'Including the charming Jean-Luc?' The question was snipped and chilled, the gaze he now directed to her face narrowed with irritation. 'You seem intimate with him.'

Surprise spiked her eyebrows. 'Who? Jean-Luc?'

His hot, probing gaze rested on her, his mouth a thin, formidable line.

Giada shrugged. 'I only met him a few days ago.'

His gaze remained on her. Narrowed. She curbed the urge to squirm. 'I don't even know his last name. I find that's the minimum basic requirement for someone I choose to sleep with.'

Dear God, why had she said that?

Something shifted in his eyes. Satisfaction? Triumph?

But even when the lights turned green and his gaze returned to the road the intensity remained, cranking up until it took complete hold of her.

'We're going to Gris-Montana,' he finally delivered.

That ended their conversation for the rest of the journey. She told herself to be thankful as they turned onto a lane marked *Propriété Privée*.

For the last twenty minutes they'd steadily climbed the mountain the area was named after, the accumulation of snow on the treetops and the landscape giving breathtaking white views as far as the eye could see.

But she couldn't stop the butterflies flapping their wings harder in her belly as the chalet came into view.

Giada couldn't suppress her gasp when she saw the structure. Partly lit by the surrounding white landscape, partly by strategically placed lights, the chalet was huge and golden and so magnificent she couldn't stop staring at it.

Made entirely of what looked like treated cedar logs, it soared against a backdrop of a snow-white mountain, a warm beacon in an otherwise chilly landscape. Wide windows broke the layers of wood and snow-topped slanting roof and, above it, a chimney sent out tufts of smoke into the sky.

It was picture-perfect and remote in the way only the super-rich could afford. The thought sent another dart of alarm through her.

Suppressing it, she turned to find Alessio examining her with the same intensity with which she'd just examined his chalet. A sardonic look followed the scrutiny, but he didn't say anything as he shoved his door open and came around to open hers.

Again, Giada was struck by his chivalry.

Again, she cautioned herself that it meant nothing.

In fact, everything she'd learned about Alessio Montaldi so far indicated that he was the kind of man who would smile and offer you your dreams on a silver platter...right before he destroyed you.

She stepped out, pulling the coat firmer around her when the freezing wind sent a chill through her. She realised she still wore his coat, and her gaze darted to him but he was walking away, her suitcase firmly in his hand.

She followed gingerly, cursing herself for not changing into the sturdy boots she'd brought. Then she reminded herself that she was playing a role. One that didn't feature sturdy work boots more suited to trudging through Antarctic snow running after penguins.

The wide breadth of his shoulders blocking the doorway stopped her from seeing the whole room save for the rich rugs that covered the polished wood floors, an opulent painting here and sumptuous velvet sofa there, until Alessio stepped aside to shut the wide door behind them.

Confronted with the floor-to-ceiling window and seeing the splendour of the snow-covered tall pines rising like giant white needles into the sky behind the chalet, Giada stopped in her tracks.

'Oh, my God, this is amazing!' The words slipped out before she could stop them. Then to cover the unguarded gushing, she hurriedly continued, 'You must love waking up to a view like this every morning?'

His shrug was cold and unaffected. 'It's a good place to own in my line of business but I rarely come here.'

He turned away and headed down a hallway that opened into another small foyer, before pausing at the bottom of the stairs leading to the first floor. 'And small talk won't be necessary, Gigi. Neither will pandering to my ego aid your cause.'

She gritted her teeth. 'You're annoyed with me. I get it. But surely, this would go more pleasantly if we made an effort to get along?'

For a moment he seemed stunned.

Then his face clouded over and the cynical amusement returned as he folded thick arms across his chest. 'Keep telling yourself that if you need to. You may think you hold a hand worth bluffing with but understand this--things *will* go my way eventually. How long you're willing to keep up this game is entirely up to you.' He looked past her and nodded. Only then did Giada see the formally dressed butler waiting discreetly a few feet away. 'Johan will show you up to your room. Come and find me in the study in fifteen minutes. We'll begin with your first task then.'

Alessio stood at the wide window in his study, irritation biting greedily at his mood. It *was* irritation, he assured himself. Any other emotion was unacceptable because that would mean he was affected by his unwanted guest. And he absolutely refused to accommodate that. Refused to assess the dash of pleasure he'd felt from witnessing her unabashed appreciation for the very view he was staring at now. The view that had swayed him into buying this chalet.

So what if Gigi Parker liked it?

Her presence was a nuisance he would delight in

doing away with as soon as possible. *Why* did he need constant reminding? As if not doing so would be…detrimental? Why couldn't he switch off his brain from recalling how soft and firm she'd felt when he'd stopped her from falling outside that deplorable place that dared name itself a hotel?

He'd performed an involuntary act he would do for most. Then he'd never wanted it to end. He'd breathed in the scent of her shampoo. Then wanted to remain exactly where he was with her locked in his arms, devouring every ounce of that glorious scent.

Diu mio, was all this snow freezing his brain? Because that could be the only explan—

The buzzing of his phone released a long-overdue growl from his throat. While he could operate from anywhere in the world, Palermo was where he thrived. It helped that it was also where his enemies were. They could cower in his presence, know the true fear of waiting for his axe to fall.

He should've put his foot down with Massimo and left days ago, he vexingly accepted, snatching his phone from his pocket.

Speak of the devil…

He read and reread his brother's text with disbelief and frustration. *'Figghiu ri—'*

'Is this a bad time?' a husky voice asked.

Alessio bit off the curse and whirled around.

She leaned in the doorway, slim arms crossed and one eyebrow raised in mild teasing. She'd changed from the cocktail dress into something equally scandalous—a pair of denim shorts that barely covered the tops of her thighs paired with a sweater that left most of her shoulders exposed and contained enough slashes and holes to render it useless. And… *Diu*…was that a neon-pink feather boa wrapped around her neck?

Had Alessio believed in the fates, he would've pleaded with them to spare him this insanity.

'I can come back later if you want?' she added, the merest wisp of amusement curving her pillowy lips.

Before he could disgrace himself with another uncustomary curse, Johan appeared, pausing a few feet from Gigi. Alessio didn't know why the presence of the butler so close to his unwanted guest riled him. Surely it couldn't be because Gigi Parker's endless expanse of killer legs was on display? Or that she followed his gaze and gifted his butler a stunning smile that made the older man's ears redden a little?

Jaw gritted, he raised his own eyebrow. *'Se?'*

His butler startled a little before inclining his head at Alessio. 'Would sir like me to serve dinner? I wasn't sure what time you would be returning but I have prepared several hot and cold meals for you to choose from.'

Alessio waved him away. 'There's no need. If everything is prepared, we'll serve ourselves when we're ready. You may leave for the day.'

If his butler was surprised by his response, he didn't show it. The older man had been employed based on his ability to exercise the utmost discretion, a trait Alessio demanded at all levels with his subordinates.

When Johan nodded and took his leave with zero fuss, Alessio sucked in a deep breath. Only to lose it again when Gigi glided into the study, her hips swaying with hypnotic rhythm he would have to be made of stone not to appreciate.

'I guess I not only need to earn my keep, I need to earn a meal too?' She stopped in front of his desk, dropped her arms and ran the tip of her finger over the polished surface. 'Then I guess we should begin.'

CHAPTER FOUR

GIADA KNEW SHE was playing with fire by goading Alessio this way.

But somewhere between leaving him in the foyer and staring cringingly at the revealing clothes she'd let Gigi talk her into packing, she'd decided that the best way forward was to keep him unsettled.

He'd agreed to her demands when he was frustrated.

He'd looked surprised when she'd admired the view from his chalet.

He'd sported a very puzzled look when he'd watched her climb the stairs to the guest room.

Somehow, for good or ill, she was doing things Alessio didn't expect. How long that remained the case, she didn't want to guess. But while he was on unstable footing, at least it would gain her some insight into how she could better deal with him.

So she'd chosen the stupidly skimpy shorts that made her insides recoil with mild horror. The sweater had been no better, with gaps that exposed most of her upper body including the skin-coloured bra she wore.

With no vest or scarf in sight, she'd had no choice but to add the feather boa to conceal *some* skin.

She looked ridiculous and felt uncomfortable. Gigi would be getting an earful the moment this infernal exercise was over.

But for now—

'What the hell are you wearing?'

The snapped query did its job of ratcheting up her unease. The seductive finger-glide stuttered and died, a tremor seizing her as she sucked in a breath.

To cover it up, she rested her hip on his desk and raised an eyebrow. 'I'm wearing *clothes*, Alessio,' she said, faking long-suffering patience.

His jaw gritted at her dry tone, but it didn't stop him from conducting a searing head-to-toe scrutiny. 'It's minus seven degrees outside.'

'Then I'm thankful you're not skimping on the heating in this lovely space.' She made a show of looking around the spectacular study, wondering whether she would get a chance to explore the floor-to-ceiling bookshelves before he tossed her out.

Gigi might abhor any literature that didn't relate to a cocktail menu but maybe Alessio didn't know that.

After several seconds' silence, she dragged her gaze from what looked like a bookcase filled with first editions to find him watching her with narrowed eyes.

Had her interest in his books given her away?

Heart dropping a little before it began thumping wildly, she straightened and forced herself to walk away from the shelves. 'Since I suspect I'm not going to win by indulging in a staring contest, shall we begin?' she pushed.

Giada had learned early on that burying one's problems or fears didn't make them go away. This situation wasn't going to get resolved until she bearded the lion in his den.

Still watching her with intense eyes, Alessio waved her to the sofas grouped in front of an exquisite fireplace. She didn't need a second bidding to relocate herself out of his direct gaze. She chose the single, sumptuous armchair, tucking one leg beneath her and quickly arranging the boa so it covered a good portion of her bare thighs.

The tingles rushing beneath her skin suggested he was still watching her but she averted her gaze, taking slow, steady breaths to compose herself.

It all proved useless when his low, deep voice rumbled across the room.

Her gaze flew up. Their eyes met.

And it belatedly registered that he wasn't talking to her. Alessio spoke with rapid-fire Sicilian into the mobile phone pressed to his ear.

Giada, being half Italian, understood enough of the conversation to know he wasn't pleased about the other person's absence, enough to glean that Alessio's growled demand for Massimo—his brother, apparently—to return immediately was falling on deaf ears.

Her cheeks burned when he uttered an earthy curse, followed by dire threats. Which didn't work, if the fingers he abruptly dragged through his hair were any indication.

Fascinated against her will, Giada watched the thick waves fall into sexy disarray as he spun around to face the window.

'This is not what we agreed, Massimo,' he gritted out in fiery censure.

Giada's breath shortened, her eyes riveted to the wide breadth of his tensing shoulders.

God, he was breathtaking.

Icily disdainful or fierily pissed off, Alessio Montaldi was captivating.

Far too captivating.

She needed to focus so she didn't mess things up for her sister. And yet, she couldn't take her eyes off him. She watched him pace in short strides, his patience rapidly fraying before he issued the final ultimatum for Massimo to present himself at the chalet by morning.

Ending the call, he tossed the phone onto the wide desk. Nostrils flared in temper, he abruptly shrugged off his jacket and tossed it over the chair.

Then those golden eyes snapped to where she sat. Without taking them off her, he sauntered close, the image of control again, as if those last minutes hadn't happened.

Giada thanked heavens she'd taken the lone seat far enough away because his very presence overwhelmed her. Stopping before the wide sectional sofa, he didn't immediately take a seat. Instead, he took his time to tug out his diamond-studded cufflinks, sliding them into his pocket before slowly folding his sleeves.

She wasn't going to stare at his brawny forearms.

She wasn't…she wasn't…she—

The flex of muscle seized her attention, the silky wisps of hair just perfect enough to make her thighs clench.

God, what was wrong with her?

Thankfully, she was saved from dwelling on the disturbing question when he folded himself into the seat and crossed one leg over the other.

Long fingers tapped his knee for several seconds. 'My client is the head of an international conglomerate.' He named the company and her eyes goggled. He saw her reaction, and one corner of his mouth twitched. 'I see you've heard of them.'

She might spend a significant portion of her time in a lab, on a research vessel or on some wide, forbidden expanse with only a handful of people, but even she'd heard of the entertainment giant. 'Anyone with a passable internet connection probably has.'

He gave a brisk nod. 'Three weeks ago he discovered that his younger brother had gambled away almost forty per cent of the revenue of the subsidiary he's in charge of and leveraged another fifteen per cent to several...unsavoury individuals.' He named the subsidiary that streamed music and videos via an app she had on her phone.

Giada's mouth gaped. His sardonic delivery made her wonder if she'd misheard. His laser eyes said otherwise. 'You're not joking, are you?'

'I rarely joke about my business, Miss Parker.'

She exhaled in stunned alarm. 'But that's...'

'Hundreds of millions and counting. And with the brother now in rehab for his gambling, the situation is enough to plunge them into serious trouble and invite an investigation from the financial authorities if it's discovered. Simply put, should this come out, it'll end the company.'

She shook her head, unable to fathom the enormity

of what he was saying. 'How did no one notice this was happening?'

Something bitterly dangerous flickered in his eyes. 'You'd be surprised how eager family are to turn a blind eye to flaws. How far they're willing to go to fool you because they know you care for them,' he said with a grating inflexion that made her tense.

Her breath locked in her lungs. Surely…he wasn't talking about her? Did he know?

Her gaze dropped to the feather boa, her fingers fussing unnecessarily with it as her brain spun. But then, her gaze slid to the discarded phone on his desk, and the snippets of frustrated conversation she'd overheard.

'Are you talking about your brother?'

He tensed, the muscle beneath his shirt rippling as he dropped his leg to the floor and leaned forward to plant his elbows on his knees. Just like in the bar, Giada was immediately aware of his power and presence. Of being the sole focus of his ferocious attention.

As if she'd ever been in danger of forgetting him, she silently scoffed.

'This isn't about me, Miss Parker.'

Are you sure?

The words hovered on her lips and she was glad she hadn't uttered them. This man had the ability to exercise supreme control, but it didn't alter the fact that, just beneath the surface, Alessio Montaldi's passions and emotions strained on a very tight leash.

For an insane second, Giada wondered what it would look like *unleashed*. Whether the very earth beneath her feet would quake with the eruption of his passions.

Thank goodness you'll never find out…

She ignored the bubble of hollowness in her belly at that thought as he continued.

'My personal life isn't up for dissection or discussion. *Caspisci?*'

His voice was a lethal blade whispering over her, dragging every nerve ending to life. It took every ounce of composure to remember she was supposed to be Gigi. Supposed to be unfazed by men like him.

'Sure,' she dismissed with an airy wave. 'I just wanted a bit more insight into the man I hope to work for.'

Derision rippled across his face. 'Counting your chickens already?'

She shrugged. 'Pessimism is a waste of good energy.'

'As is overconfidence, I imagine.'

'True. That's why I prefer a comfortable midpoint between the two. So, you were saying?'

Another flash of emotion crossed his face, this one echoing bewilderment. Giada reminded herself it was a good thing. She was keeping him unsettled.

Yet she almost regretted it when he leaned back, assuming his previous posture. 'My client wants his problems to go away before the annual board meeting in three weeks. Which also happens to be when his father turns ninety. And they announce a merger with another *FTSE 100* company.'

The sheer magnitude of the miracle he…or *she* needed to perform threatened to make her jaw drop again. It was at once exhilarating, daunting and overwhelmingly personal.

Despite their billions, a family stood on the brink of being shattered beyond repair because of the actions of a brother and son. Hadn't Gigi mentioned something about Alessio helping to orchestrate the ousting of the corrupt president of Cardosia in favour of his nephew?

Were his 'fixes' personal? Was that why he did it? What did it matter?

'Tell me how you would go about fixing it,' he invited in a silky tone, much like a snake hypnotising its prey before it struck.

Giada licked her lip, her heartbeat not at all interested in settling down. 'Well, for starters, three weeks is out of the question. I'd find a way to buy more time.'

His mouth twitched again and she found herself tracing the curve with her eyes. 'That is not an option,' he stated unequivocally.

'Then it's impossible.'

'Throwing in the towel so quickly?' he taunted. 'I guess this interview is going to be even quicker than the last one.'

He started to rise. Panic raced up her spine. 'No. Wait.'

One eyebrow rose. And he waited.

'I… I need time to consider how to go about it. And more information about the family.' She cast a glance at his bare desk. 'Surely you have a file somewhere?'

'I do. But giving you the broad strokes is one thing, disclosing the finer details of the situation is another. Not that I won't sue you for everything you possess…' he paused, his gaze raking mockingly over her attire '…and ensure you never hold a relevant job anywhere for the rest of your life, if you breathe a word of this to anyone.'

Giada shrugged as if his words didn't sting. 'I won't.

But if you like, I can sign one of those non-disclosure things,' she said, hoping he'd refuse. Gigi didn't have a discreet bone in her body, which really begged the question why she was so keen on landing a job with Alessio Montaldi.

If he was surprised by her offer, he didn't show it. Frankly, he looked bored. 'Contracts like that aren't worth the paper they're written on if one party has nothing to lose. Tell me, Miss Parker, what do you have to lose?' The words were soft, deadly, couched with more than a bite of suspicion.

'Far more than you think,' she said before she thought the better of it.

That got his attention. Glinting eyes pierced hers. 'Please. Enlighten me,' he invited silkily.

'Wouldn't that be falling under the personal label you wish to avoid?'

Touché, his expression said, but he didn't vocalise it. Nor did his gaze leave her. Whether this was his way of disarming his prey or he found her singularly of interest, Giada couldn't tell. She needed reprieve from it. While at the same time absurdly…craving it.

Since there was no way she was going to tell him that her work as a senior research scientist attached to one of the world's leading public think tanks would be seriously jeopardised should her activities come to light, she kept her lips sealed and awaited his next move.

Which was an indolent shrug interrupted by her loudly growling stomach. With another sardonic look, he rose.

Even from across the short distance between them he towered over her, overwhelming her anew. But the relief she expected when his gaze left her to flick to the window didn't arrive.

Outside, the last of the day's winter sunset broke through grey clouds to glint off the snow. But she suspected Alessio wasn't glancing out to admire the snow. Sure enough, he strode briskly to his desk and retrieved his phone, peppering the silence with a quick text.

Giada watched his lips firm when the answering *bloop* sounded. Tossing the phone back onto the desk with suppressed anger, he strode for the door, glancing at her over his shoulder.

'Come. We might as well have dinner. Perhaps you'll be more efficient once you've eaten something.' He paused with his hand on the handle. 'Unless you're in the grip of one of those fad diets that consist of alcohol and not much else?' he added.

Her face stinging with heat, she wanted to refuse his offer on principle alone. But she was starving, having barely eaten more than a ridiculously tiny but overpriced bowl of olives and cheese at the bar, and a slice of toast with coffee as her meagre hotel breakfast this morning. As much as she wanted to emulate her twin in this regard too—since Gigi could seemingly survive on air and alcohol—Giada couldn't deny the vital sustenance she needed to function.

Especially now.

Her discomfort ramped up as she recalled her mother's mockery of her voracious appetite.

'You double my food budget when you're here. Why can't you be more like Gigi?'

'Are you coming?' Alessio bit out, impatience pulsing off his body.

Giada rose, then felt even more self-conscious when the boa fell away, leaving her once more with several acres of skin on show.

Whether that was why Alessio's hand tightened on the handle or because this whole situation was highly vexing him, she chose not to examine as she crossed the room.

'Food sounds great. Thanks!'

Without replying, he walked off, leaving her to follow.

Beyond the study lay a sumptuous dining room, all twelve places set with exquisite silver-and-grey-toned tableware that complemented the soft grey velvety chairs and smoked-glass table.

Alessio bypassed it, heading deeper into the chalet, to what she discovered was a masterpiece kitchen, complete with a wide island with further places set.

As Johan had detailed, a long side cabinet held several heating domes emitting incredible aromas, while, on another side, cold dishes were served on silver platters.

The large spread gave Giada pause. 'This seems a lot for two people. Are you expecting company?' Why did the thought of him entertaining guests, maybe *a woman*, make something sharp catch in her midriff?

Alessio paused on his way to the charcuterie board holding at least ten kinds of ham, cheese, olives and mouth-watering golden tarts. He grabbed one tart and tossed it into his mouth before turning sideways to glance at her. 'Would that have stopped you from striking your deal with me?'

'Of course not. But I don't recall you cancelling any plans either, so…'

Why the question brought a bite of irritation to his face, she discovered a second later. 'My brother has been using the chalet for the last week. His guests drift in and out as they please. I didn't plan on staying this long when I arrived on Friday. He was supposed to return to Sicily with me.' His eyes sharpened. 'But then you know most of that already, don't you?' he tagged on, a chilled note in his voice.

It was one question she could answer guilt-free. 'No, I really didn't.'

Gigi had made a wild guess on Switzerland, but she'd also mentioned Alessio had winter chalets in Val-d'Isère and Aspen, all rarely used by the workaholic billionaire. She didn't know why her sister had settled on Gstaad and she was glad she hadn't asked.

Alessio slanted her a disbelieving look before turning to fill his plate.

Giada chose to remain on her side of the kitchen.

The first cloche offered up a mouth-watering dish of thick lobster bisque with warm, rich rolls, the next a stuffed vegetable pie that suffused the air with garlic and rosemary. Grilled cutlets of lamb and feta almost made her groan in delight.

She helped herself to the bisque and added a salad, then joined Alessio at the kitchen island. Since he didn't seem in the mood for further conversation, she busied herself with unfurling her napkin and pouring herself a glass of water.

Then, the aromas growing irresistible, she took the

first bite. She couldn't help herself. She moaned, indescribably good flavours exploding on her tongue.

Alessio's hand tightened around his fork, then he jerked to his feet and stalked away without a word.

Giada watched him leave, her skin jumping with trepidation. She was slowly chewing another mouthful, wondering what had happened, when he returned. She refused to acknowledge the tiny burst of relief when he held up a bottle of red.

She was no wine connoisseur but just by reading the label even she knew the rare vintage he held was worth several thousand euros.

'I'm assuming this is to your liking? If you prefer cheap champagne, I'm afraid you'll be disappointed.'

She exhaled in a rush, fire lighting her belly at his edgy dig. 'This is getting old very quickly. It's clear you're in a terrible mood but I suspect it's not all down to me and this situation we find ourselves in, so can you please stop piling on me?'

Fierce eyebrows clamped thunder on his features. 'Piling…on you?' he echoed with a puzzled rasp, fingers curling around the neck of the bottle.

The weirdest thing happened.

Giada laughed, the burst of mirth erupting from the depths of her frayed nerves.

Alessio's eyes widened. Right before his golden eyes darkened and latched onto her mouth.

'It means—'

'I have a fair idea what it means, Miss Parker,' he interjected, his voice still curiously husky. A moment later, he exhaled. 'You're correct. It's not often I let other matters get in the way of what I want.'

The admission sent shock waves through her. She didn't need to spend a considerable length of time with him to know Alessio Montaldi wasn't a man who disclosed such things freely. From his disgruntled expression, she suspected he was equally alarmed by the revelation.

He gave a brusque shake of his head and held the bottle higher. 'Wine?' he bit out.

Indecision prickled her.

She rarely drank beyond the occasional birthday or celebratory toast. And as she'd learned in the few hours she'd been in his company, she needed to keep her wits about her. But those same wits could glean quickly that she would be acting out of the norm if she refused, since her sister was a keen supporter of the 'it's five o'clock somewhere' attitude to drinking.

'If you're planning on getting me drunk then pumping me for information on your property, it's not going to work,' she said, hedging to buy herself some time.

His head snapped back, his eyes boiling with fury.

Giada wanted to rush to apologise but something held her back. The same absurd urging she'd had earlier on.

The need to see him lose control.

'I have very little doubt that you'll spill the goods sooner rather than later. And it won't involve underhanded tactics. At least not on my part.'

The last bit was aimed squarely at her and the shame that unravelled through her, heating her face and robbing her of breath, was evident for him to see.

He gave a mocking smile of acknowledgment of his bullseye strike. Then he reached for the bottle, uncorked it and poured the glass she'd so clumsily attempted to refuse.

Now with little choice if she didn't want to appear churlish—and to save her speaking and disgracing herself further—Giada snatched the glass and took an unwittingly large gulp while her mind raced for ways to extract herself from this.

Several minutes later, her senses were still swimming, and, while she suspected most of it was due to Alessio and his infernal *presence*, she knew some of it was due to the wine, too.

Watching her mother and sister make spectacles of themselves after imbibing alcohol had made her shy away from the stuff, earning her another of the myriad names they liked to label her with. But here she was, skating dangerously close to edges she normally stayed far away from.

And not just that. She was also risking giving herself away.

Thank goodness he'd given her a reprieve from the interview for dinner. She stared into her glass, wondering if he'd suspect anything if she announced she was going to bed after their meal.

Since it was barely eight p.m. that would definitely raise suspicion.

'So what else is getting in the way of what you want? Besides me, that is?' she said in the silence. Having polished off her first course, she hedged for a few minutes before deciding she wasn't going to cut off her nose to spite her face when she was dying for another helping.

Hell, if the worst happened and he threw her out, at least she'd have a full stomach.

Scooping up a helping of lasagne and adding a gooey square of garlic bread plus salad to it, she turned to find him watching her.

His gaze went from the plate to her face and Giada stiffened.

'Your appetite is more robust than I remember,' he observed with something like approval coating his voice.

She sent a quick plea that the blush creeping up her chest wouldn't reach her face. 'I wasn't aware my appetite was a thing of interest to you.'

'It isn't. But I recall you barely touching any food the last time we were in the same place together. Booze was more your speed.'

Since she didn't want to incriminate herself, Giada waved an airy hand. 'My appetite comes and goes. And when the food is this amazing, how can I resist?'

His gaze dropped to her mouth, then progressed down her throat and body. 'Interesting.'

Oh, God.

Giada turned back to the buffet to hide her dismay.

Did he believe her? Forcing her brain to stay on track, she cleared her throat. 'You haven't answered my question. And before you say it's none of my business, you opened the door.' Glad her voice was brisk with no signs of her inner turmoil, she returned to the island. 'So?'

He waited until she sat, then topped up her wine glass before she could stop him. Rising, he went to replenish his plate too, choosing giant meatballs smothered in tomato sauce, and *garganelli*. 'My brother assured me he would be here so we can return to Palermo together tomorrow for the holidays as per our family tradition.'

Something sharp knifed her gut. It felt uncomfortably like envy.

She'd stopped wondering what it would feel like to have a warm and comforting tradition set in stone, to not live with the uncertainty of wondering which whimsical place her mother would choose and what atmosphere awaited her when she inevitably dragged herself there. 'You spend holidays with your family in Sicily?'

'Se,' he responded, a bite of something earthy and solemn in his voice. 'Don't tell me, you prefer the company of a big, rowdy crowd made up of acquaintances you barely know to lose yourself in?'

She forced herself not to react because what he'd said was partly true.

Much as she'd yearned for the close comfort of her small family in years gone by, she'd come to accept that would never happen. These days Giada would much rather stay on a research vessel and work through the holidays than put herself through her mother's inevitable roller-coaster cycle of emotions. It seemed the older her mother got, the more erratic the occasions were destined to become.

'You know me well,' she quipped, assuring herself that leaning into Alessio Montaldi's stereotyped assumptions was better than revealing the stark bewilderment of her dysfunctional family.

His lips compressed, disdain reigniting in his eyes.

Giada told herself it was better this way, but she couldn't stop the hollow yawning in her belly. 'The evening is still young. Time enough for your brother to return. So what's the problem?'

'The problem is Massimo took my helicopter. And informed me by text half an hour ago that I shouldn't expect him in the morning because he's planning to spend the day with friends in Verbier. So the very earliest I can hope to leave this place is tomorrow evening.'

'And to a man like you, a few more hours in a gorgeous chalet is a fate worse than death?' she attempted to tease.

His eyes narrowed. 'When this isn't where I want to be or the company I desire? *Se*, it most definitely is,' he bit out without mercy.

Was she shocked that he didn't bother to hold back that her company was the last thing he wanted? Probably not. But she *hated* that intensifying hollowness in her body.

Because it reeked far too much of the dejection she suffered whenever she was with Gigi and her mother. She hated that she'd never managed to wrestle away the *yearning* and the *hope* and fruitless *wish* for a better connection with the only family she had. Especially during the holiday season.

There was a time in the distant past when Christmas had been a true time for joy. When her mother had come within a whisker of being happy, when Giada and Gigi had the promise of a proper family within reach. Perhaps that was why she hated this time of year. Her foolish heart never failed to *yearn*.

And reality was always, *always* worse than the expectation.

'You find my words harsh? Or just personal?'

She startled and looked up to find his gaze near her plate. Following it, she saw how tightly she'd gripped her fork.

She relaxed her fingers. 'Do you care?' she countered, pride sparking anger. 'We're using each other as a means to our own ends, aren't we? Like you said, our personal lives aren't part of the deal. My feelings in this don't matter. The fact that you might be my potential employer shouldn't change anything. You employ thousands of people. I'll do my job and we don't even need to see each other again after tonight.'

For some reason, he looked even more disgruntled. He set his own cutlery down and picked up his wine glass.

Giada couldn't stop herself from glancing at those capable fingers wrapped around the delicate crystal. Remembering how they'd felt against her skin when he'd thrown her over his shoulder and stormed out of the club in Gstaad. How his touch had branded her.

Heat rose to blend with the other sensations swirling through her. She shifted in her seat, willing them all away. But they remained, intensifying as he lifted the glass, his eyes fixated on her as he took a healthy gulp.

'I stay in constant touch with my teams. I find face-to-face interaction produces the best results. Things have a habit of…festering in the dark. Assuming things are running smoothly out of sight is asking to be stabbed in the back.'

His nostrils thinned and a shadow moved over his face as he spoke. Before she could begin to work out what that meant, he continued, 'I've learned not to allow that to happen. So should you, in the unlikely event, find yourself contracted to me, you won't have the freedom of running around thinking you can do what you want. Perhaps you should consider that before this goes any further?' There was a slice of something smug and almost...*anticipatory* in his voice.

As if he relished the opportunity to toy with his prey.

A shiver raced over her. The notion that she'd be required to be at his beck and call every hour of every day—because she suspected there was nothing as mundane as a nine-to-five with this man—*excited* her.

Well, not *her*.

Gigi.

There was that hollow again.

What was wrong with her?

Sucking in a breath, she reached for her glass of water with a touch of desperation. It would do her more good than the wine. 'That's good to know. And no, that won't change my mind. I still want this job.'

His eyes glinted with a mixture of mockery and begrudging...respect? When the latter eased a touch of that hollowness, Giada suspected that her brain and body were playing tricks on her.

Because that would mean...

She jerked away from the table, and when his eyes narrowed, she picked up her half-finished plate and headed for the sink.

'What are you doing?' he growled behind her.

'I've finished eating. And as you dismissed your butler for the night, I'm clearing up.' She shrugged, not turning around in case he read her befuddled feelings in her expression.

For several seconds, silence reigned behind her, then she heard the distinct sound of his chair scraping back.

Giada's skin tightened as he strolled closer. As his scent hit her nostrils. As he paused behind her before stepping next to her, his plate in hand.

As she felt the singe of his regard before he drawled, 'I'm reluctant to admit you've done the impossible, Gigi. You've surprised me. Whether that's a good or bad thing, I'm yet to make up my mind. Perhaps having another day I don't want freed up in my schedule may not be a bad thing after all.'

CHAPTER FIVE

HIS WORDS MADE her nervous, Alessio could tell.

For some reason he welcomed it. Relished it in fact because it eased some of the unsettled feelings rushing freely through him. And while he wanted to blame Massimo and his infuriating avoidance antics for those emotions, Alessio knew most of it stemmed from this woman.

Diu, his confession was ringing in his ears and he *still* couldn't believe he'd given his potential adversary an insight into his thoughts.

And she was an adversary. Just because she didn't seem like the entitled princess he'd initially written her off to be didn't mean he could lower his guard.

She was still withholding his property from him, after all.

But even her nervousness was a surprise.

The Gigi he'd encountered before didn't have a nervous bone in her body. She'd been the typical brazen, party-addicted socialite chasing her next adventure, not this seemingly conscientious individual who baulked at drinking wine and tidied up after herself without whining about the absence of servants.

She's playing a part…

The realisation sent a bolt of ire—and alarming disappointment—through his gut.

He watched her closely, saw her visibly relax her shoulders and breathe out, while avoiding his gaze and throwing open cabinets until she found what she was looking for—the dishwasher.

With a touch of that bewilderment that irritated him, he watched her place her dish and cutlery within, before pointedly looking at his. When he didn't move, her gaze flicked up. The hint of nerves and spark of fire within stoked his own.

A little bemused by the whole situation, Alessio—who couldn't remember the last time he'd stacked a dishwasher—stepped forward and slotted in his used plate and cutlery.

Then straightened, his hands propped on his hips.

Your move.

She licked her lower lip, then bit the inside of it as her eyes darted once more around the kitchen, avoiding his. When she spun away from him and hurried back to the stool, he couldn't help but stare at her lush behind, a groan rising forcefully in his throat before he swallowed it back down.

'I've had an idea about your problem.'

'You mean your problem, don't you?' he countered, striding after her with a compulsion he couldn't stop.

She shrugged, and while she dragged her wine glass towards her, she made no move to drink, contenting herself with running a slim finger along the edge. 'I guess. Okay, here's my idea. Since it's a subsidiary, would your client be prepared to sell it off quickly? Get rid of it so it's no longer part of the whole? Surely the new buyers would agree to take the other thriving businesses at a renegotiated deal than saddle themselves with the problematic subsidiary?'

'They probably would, if the problem wasn't being kept under strict wraps. This subsidiary forms part of the deal. Suddenly selling it off would raise more questions and invite more scrutiny. And you also forget the issue of the fifteen per cent in the control of others. That isn't a problem that can be wrapped up as neatly as everyone would want.'

'Why not? Who are these people?' she asked, her eyes wide with curiosity and speculation. 'You mentioned they were unsavoury. Just how…umm…unsavoury?'

Alessio's jaw tightened. 'They're the kind of vicious leeches who target and prey on weak individuals. The kind who shouldn't be allowed to get within a mile of someone like my client's brother, and yet it's inevitable that he'd fall within their clutches.'

He hadn't meant that to come out so forcefully. Hadn't meant to let on that crushing the kind of parasites he abhorred had been the only reason he'd taken on this particular client.

'Why is it inevitable?'

'Because people have the unfortunate habit of believing the worst can never happen to them. That they're safe trusting the best of people who lie and cheat their way into positions of power. Right up until they discover differently. Almost always by then, it's too late.'

As it'd been too late for his father, his mother and far too many members of his family. In the space of one lazy Sunday afternoon, his family had been decimated by men his father thought he could trust.

The speculation in her eyes deepened and he wondered why the hell he couldn't shut up. She didn't need to be a rocket scientist to work out that there was some *personal history* behind his clipped words.

He turned from her, stabbing his fingers through his hair as the roiling intensified within him. He'd never been great with being away from Sicily at this time of year. It had been his mother's favourite season, every moment before Christmas Day a time of joyous celebration. Even after the tragedy, despite her sorrow and heartbreak over her dead husband, she'd been determined to put on a brave front for her sons.

Of course, it also inevitably reminded him of all that had been taken from him, and reignited the vow he'd made to make his enemies pay.

Maybe that was why all these useless emotions were leaking from him.

Basta...

Massimo had better present himself tomorrow or he would hunt him down and make him regret these silly games he was playing with him.

Until then...

He turned back to her, his gut clenching again when he found her eyes pinned on him. Her expression was a mix of sympathy and heated curiosity. He hated the first, was unwillingly drawn to the second.

Alessio couldn't...didn't feel inclined to look away.

Something in Gigi Parker's eyes drew him. A spark within the smoky grey that propelled fire and need through him that had nothing to do with the turbulent situation with his brother, his client, his stolen heirloom or the outside world, and everything to do with the comprehension that he was *attracted* to her.

Diu mio. A growl left his throat before he could contain it.

She startled in her seat, but surprisingly, after a beat, said, 'Well, the only way forward that I can see is for your client to come clean or to buy off these people who own the fifteen per cent. As much as it sticks in my craw to help them profit further, sometimes it's better to cut your losses.'

Interesting. 'And if they won't go away?'

Her eyes widened into sparkling pools that he wanted to get lost in. Then a shadow crossed her face and she lowered her gaze for a second before meeting his again. 'Everyone has a price. Or barring that...'

Her voice drifted off and a look came over her face, a reluctance as she took a breath.

'Or what?'

Her lips firmed, then she forced the words out. 'A weak spot that they don't want exposed?'

Now it was his turn to burn with curiosity. The depth of feeling in her voice told an intriguing story. The need to know pounded through him, boundaries be damned.

He forced himself to suppress the need to demand to know what it was.

'You recommend that I exploit that weak spot?' he asked, quietly impressed and intrigued.

'Aren't you going to anyway?' she returned, mild challenge and...something else in her eyes.

Something that resembled... She wasn't *judging* him. Was she?

'You find something wrong with the way I fix problems, *duci*?' he asked silkily, wishing his earlier fury with her would return. Because, really, who was this creature to judge him? She was a *thief*. A common, albeit alluring, mercenary. 'Aren't you, right in this moment, playing dirty to get what you want?'

She had the grace to blush—another intriguing ability he wouldn't have believed her capable of at their last interaction. Alessio followed the pink trajectory, an urgent craving to trace his fingers along her skin attacking his insides.

'Would you have given me a chance any other way?'

'No.' Alessio didn't have any qualms about admitting it. After the harrowing experiences he'd endured, he apologised for very little. Still, he avidly watched her reaction to his response.

She shrugged. As if she didn't care one way or the other.

His disgruntlement rankled again. Along with his reluctant admiration.

This woman had a thicker skin than he'd credited her with. What else lay beneath that satin-smooth skin? His tongue thickened in his mouth as other, more carnal, demands arose.

'So are you going to?'

'*Cosa?*' he asked in his mother tongue, his thoughts firmly mired in carnal filth.

'Explore their weak spots on behalf of your client?' Her tone still held a measure of judgement.

Yes, he wanted to reply. But the pang stopped him. Which was ridiculous.

He should have no reservations about dishing out retribution where it was deserved. 'Ultimately, if that path is taken, it'll be the client's call.' Her gaze stayed on him a fraction longer, and he gritted his teeth when the pang sharpened. Enough of this. 'But whether I do or not shouldn't stop you from finding alternatives—where are you going?' he asked sharply when she pushed her glass away—still half full—and rose.

Her gaze darted to the window and the darkness that had encroached while they'd been eating. 'I'm going to bed. If we've got all day tomorrow, I'd rather approach this with a fresh perspective in the morning.'

Another jolt of shock rocked him.

She was calling it a night? *She* was taking herself off to bed when he was wide awake?

Every single, sexually available woman he knew would've taken swift advantage of the hunger he knew blazed in his eyes and thrown herself at him by now. Curiously, this woman was almost jumpy with denial and nerves she was doing her utmost to hide, her gaze darting to then away from his as he stared in blatant disbelief.

She wasn't playing hard to get.

Alessio had been well versed in that particular game since he was seventeen and navigating his way through boyhood into manhood under circumstances that would've felled a lesser man.

No, she was genuinely walking away, leaving him to cool his heels.

He wanted to deny her escape, to state unequivocally that *he* would decide when she went to bed. But even in his head, it sounded churlish and borderline childish, the actions of a weak man, and he, Alessio Montaldi, was anything but weak.

Besides, he had a few dozen tasks demanding his attention. Tasks that would ensure he didn't give this creature a single second more than he'd already wasted on her.

He'd barely managed a curt nod of dismissal when she stepped away from the island, that ridiculous boa trailing on the floor. He watched her nervously pluck at it as she stared at him, her lips moving but no words forming.

Was she rethinking her decision? Had she rightly realised she was letting an opportunity pass and was about to suggest the much clichéd and highly suggestive nightcap—?

'See you in the morning.'

Another rumble of disquiet held him still and mute. But it didn't stop his gaze from tracking her when she headed for the door.

Nor could he drag his gaze from the lush swaying of her hips, from the delicious curve of her ass and the sculpted legs he could imagine wrapping around his hips as he drove into her.

That was not going to happen! Remember who she is. Why she's here.

'Gigi.' His voice was a touch untamed, echoing his feelings inside.

Did her shoulders hitch with tension before she faced him? 'Yes?'

'My property, it is safe?' Alessio despised the throb of emotion in his voice, even more so when her eyes widened at hearing it. Perhaps that was why her gaze dropped. Why she slicked her tongue over her bottom lip.

His reputation was ruthless enough for people to believe he had no emotions. Maybe this creature had believed it too. Was he embarrassing her?

For some absurd reason, Alessio wanted to reassure her that he was human.

Thank God, he killed that notion quickly.

Her gaze rose again. 'You have my word that you'll be reunited with your property once we're done here.'

By the time she reached her room, Giada was drowning in guilt. Sagging against the door after she shut it, she took a deep breath, tried to reason with herself.

He'd asked for reassurance. She'd given it without truly knowing whether she was able to do so. But what other choice had she had?

A low moan escaped her and with every sinew in her body, she wanted to rush across the room, dig out the phone, and call Gigi. Demand to know precisely when she was retrieving Alessio's heirloom and to hell with the radio silence they'd agreed on.

But even as the thought tempted her, she knew she couldn't risk it. Aside from the threat of exposing her sister, that look on Alessio's face just now was enough to stay her hand. That tiniest sliver of vulnerability quickly doused but present enough to have made her breath catch. To have triggered a yearning to know exactly what the family crest meant to him. Why he was so desperate to have it returned to him.

Of course, she hadn't dared. She might have fast-talked her way into this position but the last thing she wanted to do was taunt the dragon.

Her gaze fell on the bed, and she moved towards it.

A quick shower and bed.

Tomorrow would be here soon enough. A day she'd have to spend in the chalet with Alessio, waiting for his brother to return.

Another moan slid free before she could stop it but, feeling a little fed up with herself for her wilting-rose performance, she straightened her spine. Crossing the room, she reminded herself that had Alessio given Gigi the full interview as he'd promised or not humiliated her enough to anger her, they wouldn't be in this situation.

He was merely reaping the consequences of his actions.

The shower was glorious, the full jets easing a few layers of her tension but by no means all of them. Giada suspected she wouldn't be able to fully relax until she left here.

Whenever that was.

The thought led to tossing and turning for hours after she slid between the sumptuous sheets. Without her phone or a watch, she had no idea what time she eventually drifted off, but she knew she'd slept way longer than usual when she jolted upright with a sinking feeling in her stomach.

The rich, heavy curtains blocking the wide windows had effectively kept the white landscape from disturbing her but she still frowned as her feet hit the floor.

Something had definitely woken her.

Padding barefoot towards the door, she pulled it

open, only to freeze when the sound of a very angry, very frustrated male reached her ears.

Giada frowned down at the flimsy nightgown Gigi had packed for her. It was barely more than a few strings of lace and netting. Shaking her head at how her sister could wear this—or any other items of clothes she owned—she gladly tugged it off and reached for the silk bathrobe she'd found in the bathroom last night.

It covered her from neck to calves more fully than anything else in her suitcase. Feeling better armoured, she brushed her teeth, pulled her hair into a ponytail and stepped out of her room.

The hallway was deserted. As were the foyer, dining and living rooms.

She hadn't actually had a full tour of the chalet so she wasn't sure where the irate conversation was taking place besides Alessio's study, which also turned out to be empty.

But as she was heading for the kitchen, she spotted the staircase leading to a lower level. And from the stairwell, she heard Alessio snapping in quick-fire Sicilian at some hapless recipient of his ire.

She debated the wisdom of bearding the lion in his den, especially without the bolstering foundation of coffee. But her feet, apparently possessing a mind of their own, propelled her down the stairs before she could stop herself.

The basement was a sublime revelation that would no doubt register properly when her attention wasn't entirely absorbed by the man pacing the heated flagstones.

As she took him in, panic of a different sort joined the roiling in her belly.

Alessio wore only a pair of black cotton lounge bottoms, sweat dripping down his very bare, very sweaty torso. The discarded boxing gloves on a bench nearby indicated what he'd been doing when he'd been interrupted.

Fireworks exploded beneath her skin and Giada was thankful her robe was thick enough to hide her body's reaction from him. Otherwise she would've needed to throw herself into the large indoor-outdoor pool sparkling invitingly just beyond a set of wide glass doors with wispy strands of steam rising off it.

Alessio hadn't noticed her yet. When he paced away from her, she gaped at the sight of his bare back, and the tattoos inked deep into his skin.

The first etching was of a sword, hilted with what looked like a ruby and emerald, with a fist clenched tight around it. Then followed a set of black roman numerals from where the tip of the blade ended, all the way down to the bottom of his spine.

It was mesmerising and she knew deep in her bones it meant something deeply personal to him. Her fingers itched to touch so badly, a sound broke from her mouth before she could stall it.

Breath held, she watched him spin around.

Alessio's flaming eyes fixed on her, his phone still glued to his ear as he rasped in Sicilian, 'This is unacceptable. I need to get out of here.'

In the throbbing silence, she heard a hesitant voice make a suggestion he evidently found displeasing, and his already statue-like form stiffened further.

'Absolutely not. You will get off the phone and find a different solution. One that doesn't involve— *Ciao?*

Ciao?' He yanked down the phone and stared at the screen, incredulity mounting on his face. '*Figghiu ri—!*' He bit off the end of the epithet, his lips thinning until they were a white tense line as he sucked in a long, sustained breath.

'I'm guessing saying good morning won't go down well right now?'

Dark eyes regarding her from beneath thunderous eyebrows, his fingers tightened around his phone. 'No, *duci*. It is far from a good morning.'

Every instinct screamed at her to leave, but her body refused to obey. 'I was about to get myself some coffee. Do you want one?'

For another uncomfortable beat, he stared at her as if having a hard time deciphering her words. Giada pivoted towards the stairs, concluding that he'd either ignore her or take her up on her offer.

She was nearing the top when she felt his presence behind her.

She concentrated on putting one foot in front of the other and thankfully made it to the kitchen without stumbling. Relieved that the elaborate coffeemaker had already been set up to dispense the heavenly nectar, she glanced over her shoulder at him. 'Double espresso?'

A flash of surprise lit his eyes before he gave a single, curt nod. While she busied herself making their beverages, he prowled from one end of the kitchen to the other.

The moment she turned with his espresso, he stopped moving, his eyes once more riveted to her. Giada didn't want to know why his singular focus affected her so viscerally.

It meant nothing. Absolutely nothing.

And yet her belly flipped as she handed him his cup. Watched him stare into its black depths for a handful of seconds before he tossed it back in one brazen swallow.

An act she found far too sexy for her sanity.

Cradling her own cup of standard coffee—if the rich smooth Java the likes of which she'd never tasted before could be called standard—she attempted to alleviate the tension whipping around the room.

'More problems with Massimo?'

Impatient irritation flashed across his face. 'I haven't spoken to my brother this morning. There's no point now.'

'Oh, I...' She frowned. 'Wait, what do you mean there's no point?'

Narrowed gold eyes bored into her, as if trying to decipher what seemed to be a ridiculous question to him. 'Have you looked outside at all?'

'Outside?' she echoed. 'No. Why would I need to—?' Giada turned as she spoke.

At first, she couldn't tell what he meant. Then, obviously impatient with her inability to grasp his meaning quickly, Alessio stalked to where she stood, took her by the elbow and marched her to the window.

Where she bore witness to the near apocalyptic white-out that stretched as far as the eye could see.

It was eerie in its beauty and terrifying in its meaning. Because she'd seen this type of snowstorm before, but thousands of miles away, in the Antarctic, where it was a run-of-the-mill occurrence. Where it was common and expected and often even celebrated from a safe distance.

But here? Now? The unwelcome implications tumbled through her head.

Her gaze flew to his, probably seeking some reassurance that her eyes were deceiving her even as she shook her head. 'No,' she breathed, her voice diminished with shock.

Which seemed to please him if the sinister smile that danced around his no longer thinned lips was an indication. 'Oh, yes, *duci*,' he stated with cold finality. 'Courtesy of a freak storm last night, we're snowed in. Which means neither you nor I are going anywhere any time soon.'

For a full minute, panic prevented her vocal cords from working. When they did, her frantic gaze returned to the window. 'That's impossible.'

The warmth of his breath brushed her ear a second before he responded, 'Not only is it possible, we're about to be hit by a harder one in the next hour. If you don't believe me, just look up.'

She did. And her stomach fell. Snow-laden clouds overhead hung thick and low, a sure sign that another fierce storm was imminent.

She sucked in a panicked breath and turned to him. 'So what's the plan? How do we get out of here?'

One sardonic eyebrow rose. 'Did you not hear what I just said?'

Because she needed space from his proximity to think and to formulate an escape—because getting cooped up in this chalet with him was *not* going to happen—she hurried to the island and braced herself against it. With her roiling insides, thoughts of caffeine no longer appealed, so she set her cup down.

Then resolutely faced him. 'But you…you're Alessio Montaldi, world-class fixer. Surely, we're not just going to sit here for…however long it takes for this to clear, are we?'

She realised she was wringing her hands when his gaze fell on them. But even as she froze the motion, he was leaning back against the very same window, toned arms folding contemplatively as he watched her. 'Why, Gigi, you seem overly agitated. Wasn't this what you were angling for all along, a chance to have me all to yourself? I thought you'd be more excited that Santa has delivered your Christmas wish much quicker than you expected or, I dare say, even deserved?'

The reminder that Christmas was fast approaching, and that she would be stuck impersonating her sister, sent bolts of panic through her.

More, her mother would be *livid* if Giada ruined whatever plans she had up her sleeves. 'Believe it or not, this isn't what I want at all.' This was supposed to have been a *brief* stalling tactic to buy Gigi time she needed to relocate Alessio's property.

His gaze hardened. 'Do you not have the courage to grab the opportunity this presents to you? Or is the distress because there's not enough of an audience here to keep you entertained? Your penchant for dancing on tables and pouring liquor down your throat does not offer the same satisfaction when you have only me for company?' he mocked.

The impulse to deny it all was swift and hot. But she forced herself to lift her chin, to stare him down with a taunting, bored gaze of her own. 'Maybe. What's wrong with wanting the company of friends? Especially around the holidays? I want this job, yes. But I also have a life beyond this. So yes, I have plans that don't include being cooped up here with you.' Her very being shook with uttering that last sentence. Because the reality grew more unnerving with each passing second.

'Except it isn't just the holidays with people like you, is it?' He tightened the screw with cynical judgement dripping from his dark gold eyes. 'Life is a year-round party, isn't it?'

She rolled her eyes. 'And you have a problem with it, I'm guessing? You'd rather everyone in the world walks around like a brute with a vendetta or some other carnage brewing in their eyes the way you do?'

Thick, charged silence rushed into the kitchen, the heartbeat drumming in her ears amplifying her foolishness. She knew it from the embers sparking to life in his eyes. From the way her fingers and toes tingled from the force of his incandescent stare. Before she could think *What would Gigi do?* Giada was rushing into speech. 'I'm sorry, I didn't mean—'

He swatted her apology away with a wave of his hand. 'I don't care what you think about me. I would happily toss you out into the storm so you can be reunited with your cheerleading squad, if your risking death didn't mean loss of my property.' He straightened and his arms fell to his sides as he strolled towards her with the false indolence and grace of a panther. 'Tell me where it is, and as soon as my team recover it, you can brave the elements back to the bright lights. Far be it for me to keep you from cheap booze and mediocre conversation.'

Oh, he was good. Breathtakingly so.

Giada's head spun with the way he'd turned the tables on her.

Her fingers knitted again—a habit she couldn't stop—and her brain scrambled feverishly. 'Who were you on the phone with earlier?' she demanded, side-tracking to buy herself time to frame an answer. 'I heard what you said about needing to get out of here. If it wasn't your brother, then who were you talking to? Was it someone who could get us out of here?' She knew her questions were too eager but she didn't care. Not if his answer was *yes*.

His pitying look said her prayers were about to be denied.

He came even closer, arms extending to rest on the countertop on either side of her hips, effectively caging her in. The scent of sweat mingled with pure man should've put her off. Instead, she had the wild desire to place her nose in his throat, *breathe him in*.

'If you heard that part, then you also heard my response. As much as you wish it, the answer is no, *duci*. The lines are down, which means no phone calls. No internet. There's no getting off this mountain. Not until the series of storms have passed. As much as we both loathe it, we're stuck with one another.'

She was absorbing the fact that Alessio Montaldi didn't find her a mere nuisance but actually *loathed* her presence when he lifted a hand.

Giada shouldn't have noticed how elegant his fingers were, with the neatly trimmed nails and the wisps of hair that dusted the back of them. But as with the tattoo that rippled and writhed with each movement, she was completely absorbed.

So much so, she didn't…*couldn't* utter a word as he slowly traced her bottom lip with his forefinger. As his piercing gaze absorbed every flicker of expression as if it were his due. As her body trembled and roused with eagerness at his electric touch and she had to scramble madly to prevent the moan that eagerly rose to her throat from escaping.

'So tell me, are you going to play a good little houseguest or are you still intent on taking a chance with the elements?'

Since she wasn't stupid and since she of all people knew first-hand how dangerous the ice could be, no matter how entrancing it was to look at, she had little choice but to give him her answer. 'I'll stay,' she said, but the next words were unplanned, falling from her lips without her permission. 'But nothing has changed since yesterday. If you're expecting meek and mild, you're going to be very disappointed.'

She'd held her breath, anticipating his displeasure or temper.

Alessio had just stared down the blade of his nose at her, that disdain surging to full force. The next instant he straightened and exited the kitchen without a word.

Leaving her to stagger back to the window, disbelief still deadening her limbs at the situation she'd found herself in.

How the hell would she survive days in this chalet with Alessio Montaldi?

And why did it send a flurry of *excited* butterflies through her belly?

CHAPTER SIX

THAT HAD BEEN three hours ago.

Alessio didn't make an appearance when she ventured out of her room and, unable to sit still with her senses jumping over the nerve-shredding situation she found herself in, she toured the rest of the chalet.

It was much bigger than she'd initially realised.

Besides the kitchen and dining areas, she discovered another, larger living room towards the back of the chalet, complete with two fireplaces, enough seating for a very large gathering, and—breathtaking enough to stop her in her tracks—a white ceiling-grazing Christmas tree, decorated exclusively with dark gold and the occasional dark green ornaments she was certain didn't come from a high-street department store.

Venturing closer, she noticed that the larger adornments contained small velvet boxes with discreet designer labels of famous jewellers giving a strong hint as to their contents.

Giada's eyes widened as she skirted the base, quickly losing count of how many such baubles graced the stunning tree. Over the mantelpieces was even more jaw-dropping opulence, little expensive gifts cleverly hidden within the strings of Swarovski crystals expertly trailed through the holly wreaths and the remaining decorations.

Had she been here under other circumstances, she would've been thrilled to explore some more. But Giada couldn't stem the trepidation pulsing through her and the one thought pounding in her brain.

She was stuck here with Alessio Montaldi. No end in sight.

The thought eventually drove her back to her bedroom, frantically looking for a way out. All that greeted her when she looked out of the window was the last snow dump two hours ago, and the promise of more in the laden skies resting over the valley.

A sound of apprehension-laced frustration erupted before she could quell it. Which made her berate herself. Since when did she dissolve into a helpless puddle at the first sign of adversity?

Since you were locked in with a man who makes your pulse skitter like loose marbles tossed on a stone floor!

Enough.

Going to her suitcase, she dug out her phone, a pang of regret piercing her. She should've texted Gigi last night instead of playing it extra safe. Powering it up, she paced her room, praying for a single bar.

After a futile half-hour, she gave up and turned it off again.

Before she'd put it away, the butterflies were kicking around again, her senses jumping. She discovered the reason why when she stepped out of her room and found Alessio in the hallway.

He'd showered and changed, but evidently it'd done nothing to ease the stark displeasure etched into his face.

She'd known she couldn't avoid him for ever, much as she wished to. But knowing didn't prepare her for coming face to face with him again. For the flurry of excitement that rushed through her when he moved closer.

Her breath caught and held as he examined her much like the specimens she pored over on her research missions. He didn't care that time grew uncomfortably long between them, nor did he give an inkling as to what he was searching for.

Whether he was satisfied at finding it or he gave up, he turned away, leaving Giada to expel a silent, pent-up breath.

'We may be temporarily stranded here but there's no reason why we can't pick up where we left off last night,' he said.

For another charged moment, her thoughts flew helter-skelter, until she realised he was referring to his client's problem. To the interview she was purportedly here for.

'Oh. Yes, of course.'

He strode a few steps away, then paused when he realised she wasn't following. 'Are you coming?'

Her gaze flew up from where it'd dropped to his backside. One eyebrow arched, his mocking eyes landing on her scorched cheeks.

Oh, God...

Had she really been checking him out as if he were a side of prime beef? Flinging her gaze to a point over his shoulder, she tried not to trip over her own feet as she followed him downstairs, and into the kitchen.

'There's more than enough from last night or fresh

cold meals in the fridge for lunch. Are you okay with vichyssoise and a salad to follow?' he asked over his shoulder.

She nodded hurriedly. 'Of course.' When she found herself watching him avidly again while he performed the mundane task of pulling dishes out of the fridge, Giada shook her head. 'I'll go and set the table in the dining room, unless you want to eat in here?'

'The dining room will do. But the table is already set,' he murmured.

She hid her grimace as she remembered seeing it before. 'Oh…yes.'

'Feel free to choose wine. The cellar is through there.'

She followed his direction and went past an industrial-sized pantry stocked to the gills with enough food to feed an army for several months.

Praying fervently they wouldn't need more than a fraction of it, Giada went through swinging doors into another room stocked brim-full of wine and spirits. Red, white, and everything in between flashed at her, leaving her with a momentary pang of disquiet. Every bottle looked vintage but, like last night, their exclusivity screamed at her. Indecision made her pluck out and return several bottles, her lip caught between her teeth.

'Problem?'

She jumped, her heart lodging in her throat, to find Alessio disturbingly close behind her. In the enclosed space, his scent assailed her, the combination of fresh ocean breeze and virile man wrapping its intoxicating effect around her.

Shifting away before he saw how her nipples had

peaked, how she was struggling to breathe, she shook her head, brazening it out. 'Not at all. I was just deciding which white to choose.'

Facing the wall of chilled vintage whites, Giada went in blind. 'This one, I think.' She pulled out the Chardonnay and passed it to him.

Alessio stared at the label with another arched eyebrow, while she fought not to squirm. 'Interesting choice.'

Unsure whether he was mocking her, she blurted, 'Why?'

He displayed the label to her and she read it properly. 'Maison de Montaldi. You have your own label?'

His mouth twisted in that musing way that wasn't pleasure nor displeasure. 'It was payment from a particularly grateful client. I look forward to tasting if it was worth it.'

'You mean you were given a vineyard as payment, and you've never even bothered to try the wine?'

He shrugged and waved her towards the door. 'I'm more partial to Sicilian wine. My French client was nearer this side of the border, which was why I had it sent here. This is only my second time visiting here since so, no, I've never had a chance to try it.'

She frowned as she preceded him out of the kitchen and down the hall to the dining room.

Once they sat down, Alessio opened the wine and poured her a glass. He twirled his own glass as she helped herself to a bowl of vichyssoise and warm bread, nodding imperiously when she indicated his own bowl.

She served him, then found herself waiting with bated breath as he sampled the wine, then shrugged.

'It's decent enough.'

Giada tried not to roll her eyes at the dry response, even while a part of her eased and dared to hope that this enforced proximity might not be so hellish after all.

The melon, prosciutto and pea salad that followed was mouth-watering. But the *pièce de resistance* was the tray of chocolate truffles he slid towards her after they'd taken their used dishes to the kitchen.

It was so heavenly it drew a small moan of delight from her.

When he stiffened and a wave of something intense washed over his face, she hurried to dissipate the approaching turbulence.

'How long have you had this place?'

He waited a beat, then, 'Six years.'

'You've only visited the chalet twice in six years?'

'I will endure it if I must, but I prefer warmer pastimes to skiing.'

'Which begs the question, why buy a remote chalet in a country that prides itself on its winter activities if you don't even like it here?' she asked.

His eyes rested on her puzzled face for a moment, as if gauging if her interest was genuine, then he nodded behind her.

'You see that mountain behind you?'

She turned and looked out of the window at the stunning view. Through the falling snow, she saw the large silhouette rising into the sky. 'Yes.'

'I own it.'

Her eyes widened. 'You own it? The whole mountain?'

'And the village. And every tree, stream and building in the five-mile radius. But I bought this place primarily for the mountain. On the infrequent occasion the mood takes me, I know I can ski without being disturbed.'

Giada realised her mouth was gaping and hastily closed it when she caught his amusement. 'Shouldn't… isn't there some sort of law against being so…?'

'Yes?' he encouraged when she paused. 'A law against wanting privacy for myself and the clients who need it? Against bailing out a micro-economy that was at risk of being exploited by commercialism?'

Surprise popped like a cork in her brain. 'You mean you saved this place?'

He shrugged. 'It was in danger of becoming a mini Verbier or Val-d'Isère. I stepped in and stopped it.'

'And yet somehow I don't think you did it solely out of the goodness of your heart,' she ventured dryly before she could stop herself.

His teeth flashed in a shark-like smile and her breath caught, both at his breathtaking male beauty and at the fact that the gesture didn't reach his eyes. 'Do megalomaniacs love boasting that they skied on *my* private mountain? And do they get charged ridiculous sums for the privilege? *Assolutamente.* There's no law that says I can't make millions while saving a small corner of the planet, too. Not *capitalising* on that is just pure naïveté, *cara.*'

She hated that his argument was sound. That he was finding ways to shatter her preconceived notions about him. Hated that all the reasons she shouldn't find this magnetising man attractive were being blown to smithereens. And that her reactions were getting stronger by the minute.

As she wrestled with her feelings, he tilted his head

to one side, studying her with a shrewd look in his eyes. 'Am I turning out not to be…what did you call me? A carnage- and vendetta-loving brute?'

Heat surged into her face and her gaze danced away from his, the look in his eyes too intuitive to engage with. His low laugh had the desired effect of raising her hackles, though. Her chin went up before she could register that a part of her enjoyed this challenge, this parry and thrust with him. Maybe a little bit too much. 'I only go on what I see.'

'Do you? And yet you condemn me for doing the same?'

Thrust.

Her soft gasp at the low condemnation drew a smile, this one more circumspect. Perhaps even a touch pity. Before she could take offence, he continued. 'I don't blame you. It happens. My job title is ambiguous enough to draw certain preconceived notions and, I dare say, intrigue.'

She couldn't deny it. She *was* intrigued. Just as she'd been astounded by her sister's interest in being in this man's orbit.

The urge not to dwell on just how intrigued she was pushed her into speech. 'How did you become a fixer, anyway? As far as I know there's no degree course for it in mainstream education.'

One corner of his mouth quirked, then his face grew serious. Solemn.

Giada even thought she spotted a flash of bleakness before it disappeared. Suddenly, the lightness in the room was gone. Her heart hammered steadily as she wondered whether he would answer.

He set his wine glass down, but his fingers remained wrapped around the delicate stem. 'From a very young age, my father drilled into me the advantage of being useful. To those with power, sure, but also to those without. There was no telling when the people who served you might be swayed away from you by someone with more power. If you treated everyone equally and with respect, you were always guaranteed loyalty, no matter what.' His mouth twisted and harshness etched with grief on his face. 'A good enough lesson, but unfortunately not one everyone ultimately believed in.'

'What do you mean?'

One shoulder rolled, as if the memory unsettled him. When he dragged his fingers through his hair, Giada got her first glimpse of a ruffled Alessio. 'People can be swayed by other things besides power and respect. They can be swayed by greed and jealousy. By the need to inflict cruelty. My father found out the hard way when he was betrayed by people he trusted. They colluded to lure him into a trap, and he paid the ultimate price.'

Not for a single moment had she expected the conversation to turn so dark and heart-rending. Or for the urge to offer sympathy to be so forceful. 'Oh. I'm sorry, Alessio.'

He stiffened for a moment, his glance finding hers and staying, a look she couldn't quite fathom. Dismay? Surprise? Acceptance? *'Grazie.'* The response was low and husky.

For the next minute, he did nothing but stare at her, as if trying to work her out. Tension slowly wound its way through her.

Had she given herself away somehow?

She swallowed, casting around her mind desperately for something to dilute his intense scrutiny. But the only thing that came to mind was the subject they were discussing. 'Does that mean you don't agree with the lessons your father tried to teach you?'

He exhaled, his gaze moving slowly over her face once more before he answered. 'Not at all. But there was one ingredient I wish he'd taken into account when practising what he preached. Perhaps he would still be alive today.' There was bitterness and a touch of *longing* in his voice she couldn't miss.

'What lesson?' Giada asked, the need to know this man more digging deeper into her.

One curve of his mouth twisted. 'Trust but verify. Or some words to that effect, I think the saying goes.'

'But you don't trust easily.'

He didn't refute it. 'Or rarely at all,' he confirmed. 'I find it serves me better that way. Blind trust is an exercise for fools.' The certainty of those harsh words sliced across her skin, as if his words were personal when they absolutely shouldn't be.

Beyond this elongated, enforced moment in time, they would never set eyes on one another again. Never share a meal or wine or the pain that resided deep in their souls.

And yet… 'You can't go through life that way,' she muttered, almost compelled to reach for a ray of light. To what? Guide him away from his pain? What right did she have?

'Can't I? Tell me, Gigi. Who do you trust?'

Caught firmly between the curious ache in her chest from hearing him call her by her sister's name, and the vastly exposing nature of his question, Giada could do nothing but shake her head and drop her gaze, desperately buying herself time to think.

They were long past frivolous discussions of wine and capitalism and mountains. Now they were venturing into territory that lay too close to her heart. Subjects that could bruise and torment.

And while she stalled, he leaned closer, mockery gleaming in his eyes. 'You see? Taking advice isn't as easy as doling it out, is it, *duci*?'

She boldly met his gaze. 'Maybe not. But I don't write people off before I allow myself the chance to know them.'

Dark amusement returned. 'Is that aimed at me? Would you like to know me better, *bedda mia*?' His husky tone thickened, morphed into something else. Something that stirred her blood in a different way. They were ricocheting between subjects with dizzying speed.

She opened her mouth to steer things back to safer ground, but different words tumbled from her lips. Words she hadn't for a single moment anticipated. 'What's wrong with that? It's not like we're going anywhere in a hurry.'

'Are you ready to expose yourself in return?' he challenged, his eyes fixed squarely on her.

Her breath strangled in her lungs. In the short time since they met, she'd witnessed myriad expressions from the formidable Sicilian. The look he cast her now cut through all the previous ones, as if he'd been toying with her before and was now revealing his truth.

Or hers.

Dear God, did he know? If so, how?

Had their phone service been restored without her knowing and he'd somehow discovered her real identity?

'I… I don't know what you mean.'

He continued watching her with those laser eyes. 'Perhaps I'm finding your whole…enthusiastic approach to working with me still too good to believe. I'm still trying to discover what happened to the "work less party always" woman I met a few months ago.'

She just about managed to pull off a flippant shrug. 'Maybe she's wised up to the fact that there are other forms of fulfilment in life? Speaking of which, should we discuss your client?' she tossed in, praying she would distract him even as she sensed that Alessio Montaldi wasn't a man who allowed himself to be distracted very easily.

When his gaze swept down and a corner of his mouth lifted, she held her breath, certain he'd seen through her ploy. When dark gold eyes returned to hers and he nodded, she sensed too that he was merely humouring her. 'Very well.'

She licked her bottom lip and tried to gather her thoughts. 'I don't think there's a way for your client to get out of this without taking some pain. You mentioned his father's ninetieth birthday is approaching. Didn't he start the company?'

Alessio nodded. 'Above a Chinese takeout shop in Brooklyn several decades ago.'

'Then get him to announce that he's holding onto the ailing company out of nostalgia until his death, at which point it'll revert to the new buyer at a discounted rate. Just buy your client some time to fix what's gone wrong. Everyone loves a bargain. And if you link it to a huge PR event with his birthday celebrations, there's a lower risk that the buyer will walk away without seeming greedy or losing face.'

When that rousing gleam entered his eyes, Giada told herself not to react. Not to squirm with anticipation at his response.

And when he rose and plucked up the bottle of wine, strolled lazily behind her to top up her glass, she ordered her breath not to stall, her senses not to glory in his nearness.

But it was all useless.

Because when he lingered after he was done with refilling her glass, with one hand on the table and his body bent over hers, every cell in her body screamed to a new dizzying layer of life.

Which only intensified when he murmured low and hot in her ear, 'There should be punishment for hiding this level of brilliant strategic thinking beneath gaudy clothes and cheap champagne, *duci*.'

Giada was desperately attempting to calm the runaway heartbeat that pulsed in her chest and between her legs when he abruptly left the dining room.

It was one thing being a billionaire with clout.

But when that clout couldn't be exerted because said billionaire was combating Mother Nature, not even the world's best fixer could win.

So for the next two days, Giada watched Alessio grow increasingly disgruntled as the blizzard raged on and off with frustrating frequency, while they warily skirted each other, sharing meals in near silence before he stormed off.

Giada suspected too that his revelations during their dinner had been more personal than Alessio had intended. While *she* couldn't replay every moment of it without her heart, mind and body reacting in varying degrees of intensity that shocked her, forcing her to scramble for a distraction.

On the fifth day, seeking another form of distraction, she walked into the basement level at sunrise, intending to wake herself up with a vigorous swim…to find Alessio had beaten her to it.

Every self-preservation instinct shrieked at her to turn and walk away, return when the coast was clear.

But firstly, she was over walking on eggshells around him. It wasn't her fault they were stranded here. Okay, maybe not totally. If he hadn't chased her down in Gstaad, he might've boarded the helicopter with his brother.

Secondly, the way Alessio moved in the water was almost transcendental in its splendour.

His powerful strokes were hypnotising, making her footsteps slow but not stop entirely as she was propelled to the edge of the sparkling pool.

Whether he was totally oblivious to his audience or knew she was there and was ignoring her—her money was on the latter—he kept swimming for another five laps. Her bet proved right when he stopped directly in front of her.

She stiffened, expecting more of the chilly atmosphere they'd inhabited for the last few days. Instead, he stared at her with open interest. Not warm, but not frosty either.

Then he took in the swimsuit she wore under her parted robe and jerked his head at the steps leading into the pool. 'Get in. I'll race you.'

Shock tightened her midriff before she grimaced. 'That's hardly fair, is it? I was just watching you. I know how fast you are.'

The glint in his eyes made her yearn to know what he was thinking. 'Maybe not. But life isn't fair. I'll tell you what, let's make it interesting. I'll give you a two-lap head start for a five-lap race.'

Was it insane that she'd expected something entirely different? Something more…daring?

His eyes gleamed some more as he watched her, the dark gold stare seeming to decipher her thoughts. 'And when I win…'

Her breath caught. 'What happens when you win?'

'I will demand something from you that you'll willingly give.'

'What happens when I win?'

He shrugged. 'You will demand the same of me.'

Her eyes bulged, the tiny fireworks beneath her skin igniting faster. 'That's…' she paused and frowned '…surprisingly broad but weirdly acceptable.'

His lips twitched in a smile that said only he knew the kind of web he spun, just as he was sure it would eventually capture her.

It was a warning she needed to heed.

And yet, her feet propelled her to the edge of the pool, then down the steps, all while he watched, his eyes devouring every inch of her skin as if he had a right to it. *To her.*

He remained at the deep end, content for her to swim to him. Giada was aware the wild beating of her heart wasn't great for a race that hadn't even started, but she couldn't calm it.

Couldn't do more than remain poised beside him, ignoring the danger signs lurking in his eyes. 'Ready?' he drawled.

She licked her lips, the water she was treading gliding over her body like cool silk. 'Yes,' she breathed.

He nodded, then remained silent for a fistful of heartbeats. Before, 'Go,' he ordered, his words just about a silky murmur.

Giada struck out with one huge breath held in, exhilaration kicking in as her year-long training for her recent Antarctic trek gave her a burst of speed that surprised her. She made it to one end on a single breath, then back to where Alessio waited on another.

She barely glanced at him as she reversed direction, but she knew the exact moment he joined the race, his powerful strokes creating mini tsunamis as he passed her on his first lap.

Unsurprisingly, he easily passed her on the last lap, strong arms cleaving through the water, and by the time she finished he was waiting for her, one eyebrow arched and his hand slicking back his hair.

Her helpless gaze followed the sleek play of muscle, her mouth watering at the drops of water that lovingly clung to his face and torso. 'Is this where you tell me I made a bad deal?'

'This is where I tell you I'm impressed. I knew I would win but perhaps not by such a small margin.'

The curiosity in his tone was wrapped around a question. One she couldn't answer in truth. Buying herself time by dipping her head back and smoothing her hands over her wet hair, she shrugged. 'I love to swim. I try to get to a pool as often as I can.'

His eyes narrowed a fraction, and her insides tightened. 'Interesting. I don't recall that about you.'

'It must be something to have perfect recall about everyone you meet. You must tell me how that feels some time.' She'd meant it to be offhand, but it emerged a touch frantic and breathless.

Desperate to salvage what could turn out to be a costly mistake, she turned away, trying not to cringe at the silence that trailed her. She felt his gaze on her as she left the pool, snagged a towel and headed for the sauna, her skin jumping with hyperawareness.

She'd barely taken a calming breath when he entered.

Against the backdrop of soft golden maple that lined the sauna, his bronzed skin rippled with vitality. And in the close confines of the heating space, there was nothing she could do but stare.

'Careful, *bedda mia*. I'm discovering that your occasional…prickliness intrigues me.'

'And I should be careful because…?' God, what was wrong with her? She should be keeping things between them strictly professional. Instead, she was openly baiting a restless lion.

'Intrigue is the one thing I can't resist.'

With monumental effort, she glanced away from him, reaching for the wooden ladle to scoop out water and toss it on the sizzling coal. Its sibilant hiss filled the enclosed space with wonderful steam and made her break out in fresh sweat.

She felt it drip down her throat and into her cleavage. Felt the almost inevitable tightening of her nipples as Alessio's gaze followed several drops of perspiration, her skin tingling as his stare slowed on the very visible signs of her arousal. 'Or it could be extreme boredom,' she said.

'You have my word that boredom is the last thing I feel right now.'

The sound that escaped made her cringe and shiver at the same time. Made her thighs squeeze together as need pounded through her, settling low in her belly and dampening her already soaked suit further.

Her fingers dug into the wood beneath her thighs, her gaze fighting not to catch his. The wisest thing was still to leave. So why couldn't she just get up and go?

'Look at me, *duci*,' he commanded in a low, deep voice.

Of course her body moved of its own accord, angling towards where he sat within arm's reach. Not nearly as far away as she needed him to be. She couldn't stop her tongue from flicking out to bathe her lower lip, then her teeth from sucking that same tingling piece of flesh into her mouth and worrying it the way she craved to worry his.

The towel he'd tied around his waist did nothing to prevent her from seeing how...*affected* he was too.

When her gaze rose again to meet his there was a hint of affront. As if her daring to call him bored greatly offended. 'You know the power of your allure. Don't insult either of us by belittling it,' he condemned in a soft, deadly tone.

Giada's jaw dropped. 'I…you…' Her brain froze as words failed her.

She was fully aware of how mentally dextrous this man was, and yet, once again, he'd pulled the rug from beneath her with a handful of words.

Words that veered heavily on the carnal but weirdly touched some soft and vulnerable place inside her. A place that needed an odd little accolade just like that.

She was a good researcher, knew that her place on any expedition team was valued, that her colleagues respected her work.

But in her private life, bolstering overtures were sorely lacking.

Knowing she affected such a powerful man, even on a purely physical level, felt like…nothing she'd experienced before. It provided balm and confidence, a thrill and yearning.

And it kept her in place when he lowered his feet to the floor, his eyes immobilising her as he crossed the small space in a single stride. As he placed both hands on the bench beside her and leaned in close until their noses almost touched and his breath washed over her parted lips.

'You have me at your mercy. Granted, it will be fleeting. So…' That infernal brow arched once more, golden eyes turned even darker with his turbulent mood, daring her.

To what?

To shatter every last crumb of self-preservation? Or grasp a once-in-a-snowstorm opportunity to know what it was like to taste a live wire of a man who made the world shake with his very presence?

Alessio's gaze dropped to her mouth, his tongue mimicking her own action a moment ago. Another whimper escaped and Giada chose to...

Shatter.

Their lips fused like a perfect, hot clay mould. Pressing, shaping, gliding and battling, she didn't know where their lips started and sensation ended as the tension of the past few days exploded in a flurry of clutching limbs and exploring hands.

Alessio pressed closer, easily prying her knees apart and slotting himself between her thighs. His towel and her swimsuit were scant barriers as he unerringly found the heated place between her legs and pressed himself against it.

A hoarse cry left her throat.

Fingers that had been eagerly exploring his hard, smooth muscles dug into his flesh as desire spiked her blood. He groaned against her mouth, a staccato burst of words smashed into incoherence between them as one hand found her breast.

Mercilessly, he pinched her nipple, then soothed it with his fingers as his tongue delved deeper. Heat built and strained and threatened to burst with their climbing need.

When Alessio's hand landed on her backside and used it to propel her even closer, her vision blurred. The edge of the cliff beckoned. All it required was friction of clothing, a thrust of clever fingers or—she shuddered at the very exhilarating thought—the tugging aside of inconvenient fabric, to experience the utter bliss of skin-on-skin contact in its most visceral form.

Giada passed these reckless but enticing thoughts through her brain and when the response was a *yes, yes, yes*, her fingers spiked into his hair, clinging on as he pushed her nearer the precipice.

'Diu mio, Gigi,' he muttered hoarsely.

She flinched, the iced water of reality that was her sister's name uttered into this space, this unique experience, yanking her back from the edge.

Giada pushed at his shoulders and when he stumbled one step back, she slapped her thighs shut, her breath puffing in desperate pants. Aware he was watching her, perhaps even puzzled by her reaction, Giada kept her gaze averted.

Sidestepping him, she hurried to the door of the sauna. And then, because the last thing she wanted or needed was for him to follow her, she paused. 'Your world may be unconventional but even I know it's a terrible idea to sleep with one's potential boss. That…' She clenched her belly, wondering why the words were painful to get out. 'That was a mistake. It won't happen again.'

The slightest hardening of his features was the only indication that he'd found her words objectionable. Lazily, he tugged off his towel and tossed it away, leaving snug trunks that left no doubt how affected he'd been by their encounter.

Still watching her, he sat down on the bench, then went one better and *reclined*, totally uncaring that his arousal was on full display.

'Tell yourself that if it aids your pitiful little retreat,

piccolo fiore. But we both know you'll bloom for me again before long. Now go, you're letting all the cold air in.'

She didn't move, those words he'd said to her before the recklessness started ironically granting her the much-needed shot of confidence. She used them to straighten her spine, to let her gaze drift boldly over his body, deliberately lingering over his crotch.

'You'll survive a little cooling down. Looks like you need it. And no, I won't be blooming for you again. I've had a taste. Once is enough, I assure you.'

She turned and strode off, her face burning when, a few steps later, his soft laughter reached her ears.

CHAPTER SEVEN

FIRST BLOOD TO HER.

Alessio begrudgingly handed her the rare prize of shattering his concentration when, hours after the sauna incident, he found himself staring into the middle distance, reliving those glorious few minutes.

He growled under his breath when his body eagerly responded to the recollection of her scent, her kiss, the noises she'd made. Of how eagerly her fingers had sunk into his body, and the way she'd rolled those supple hips against him.

He still didn't understand her abrupt retreat. And something about what she'd said about putting professional distance between them didn't ring true. Especially when she knew his way of doing business was unconventional at best.

A laugh escaped him.

To think the thief who still held his possession hostage would dare to lecture him on professional etiquette?

It was maddening. But...*exhilarating*.

He tossed his pen away and surged to his feet, his temper worsening when his gaze landed on the snow falling relentlessly outside the window. He'd flicked on one of the many TVs in the chalet an hour ago and swiftly turned it off when the forecast had predicted nothing but more snow.

On his desk were a dozen urgent situations requiring his attention. And yet, he couldn't dwell on a single one, never mind attempt to resolve it, without the enigma of Gigi Parker rippling through his concentration like a stone dropped into a pond.

Alessio frowned, something irritating the back of his mind.

He was missing something. But what?

A chime erupted, deepening his frown.

Then he was spinning around, registering the sound as real and not in his head. He powered his laptop in time to watch dozens of messages flood his inbox, but it was his phone he reached for.

Massimo's message that he'd returned to Sicily triggered both relief and irritation. At least *one* of them would be at home for Christmas.

One of them would visit his mother's grave with her favourite flowers and to leave a box of Cuban cigars their father had been partial to at his tombstone. He wasn't so sure Massimo would renew the vow Alessio made to their parents each time they visited their resting places, but he could only hope.

He sent a curt reply to Massimo, his mood on being stranded here not calm enough for him to deal with his brother over the phone just yet.

The next message was from the head of his top team promising a fuller report on Gigi Parker within twenty-four hours. His irritation mounting at the disorganisation he suddenly found himself surrounded with, he read the remaining messages, including the one from his American client.

Appeased this was something he could control and resolve, he dialled the client's number, relaxing in his seat as it was answered on the first ring.

'I've been trying to reach you for days,' the harried CEO said. 'Do you have a solution for me? The potential investors are threatening to call off the deal.' The man sounded desperate to the point of pleading.

Alessio paused for a second, the solution he'd intended to provide drying up on his tongue. Instead, he found himself offering up the solution Gigi had suggested, a strange mix of alarm and pride surging through him when the man enthusiastically embraced it.

'Yes. I'll get my PR machine on it right away. I've already told my father what's happened, and he'll be on board with this. You're a miracle worker, Montaldi.' Relief heavily laced his laughter. 'I've been getting ready to throw in the towel and risk tanking this deal, but not any more. I owe you big. Besides your fee, of course.' He laughed again.

Alessio gripped the phone, gritted his teeth before he confessed, 'You owe me nothing. It was a member of my team who came up with it.'

'Well, whoever they are, I'm happy to meet them when this is all over, express my thanks in person and pass on that favour. They're saving me and my family from a potential hostile takeover and being dragged through the tabloids.'

Pure, unadulterated jealousy jolted him, as alien as it was shocking. The idea that the woman currently trapped in the chalet with him could soon be free to accept accolades and gifts from men like this grateful CEO made a muscle throb at his temple.

Inferno, he wasn't a caveman. He knew and worked with impressively clever and formidable women. Had bedded several, in fact.

And yet he couldn't pinpoint what it was about Gigi that made him feel as if he wanted to delve ever deeper into her very soul and mind, while simultaneously devouring every inch of her delectable body.

Basta.

His body was reacting to a longer than usual absence of physical stimulation. As soon as he left this frozen hellscape, he would indulge until this hunger in him abated. A holiday gift to himself, perhaps.

But even as the thought formed, he was dismissing it in distaste. Just as he was begrudgingly accepting that the chalet wasn't so bad. There was a certain… freedom from being suspended from the pressure to act. To fix. *To avenge.*

It would return soon enough, he knew.

But perhaps for now, he could just *be.*

With her.

Alessio dragged frustrated hands down his face as the infernal hunger prowling within grew, demanding satisfaction. Demanding to see her.

'Like I said, that won't be necessary,' he reiterated, noting that his voice was edged in cold steel.

Silence pulsed at the end of the line before the other man cleared his throat. 'Sure, understood. I'll be in touch to let you know how it goes.'

'You do that.' He hung up and realised his other fist was bunched.

Consciously unfurling his fingers, he rose again from his seat.

Alessio wasn't sure why he felt the urge to inform Gigi that her solution had been well received, especially since he was still annoyed by how their interaction in the sauna had ended. And yet, he found himself mounting the stairs and heading down the hallway towards her room.

The sound of her low, agitated voice when he got close quickened his footsteps to her open bedroom door.

She'd obviously noted the internet connection was back because her phone was pressed to her ear, her fingers dragging through her long ash-blonde hair as she listened for a moment, oblivious to his presence.

The look on her face before she turned towards the window made him freeze in the doorway, the very strong urge to cross the room to her side and demand to know what was upsetting her shocking him into stillness.

Because these strong feelings he was experiencing around her? They needed to be killed.

Sooner rather than later.

'No, Renata, I didn't plan it. I may be capable of many things but even I don't have the power to command snowstorms.' Sarcasm was rife in her voice but then so was the throb of pain and distress behind it.

'Why do you even want me there? All we're going to do is disagree…no, I'm incapable of predicting the future, but it's a reasonable assumption when the same pattern repeats…' She paused and took a breath as a torrent of English-laced Italian ranted down the phone.

'Well, you're just proving my point. I'm already

aware I'm a disappointment to you. Maybe it's a good thing I can't make it for Christmas. You can enjoy yourself without my disappointing presence to spoil the holidays.'

Another deluge shot through the handset, making her flinch.

The growl Alessio couldn't quite halt caused her to turn, stiffen, then pale as she saw him in the doorway.

'I… I have to go. Goodbye, Renata.' A look he couldn't quite decipher shot across her face as she glanced frantically around, as if searching for…or hiding…something. Then she speared him with furious smoky-grey eyes. 'Does the word privacy mean nothing to you?'

'Who's Renata?' he bit out before he could stop himself, ignoring the return of the tingling that insisted that he was missing something.

More shadows drifted across her face, and he gritted his teeth at her momentary look of desolation. 'She's no one I wish to talk to you about,' she answered, her beautiful chin raised in a challenge that made his blood hotter.

Santo cielo, did anything about this woman not fire him up?

'You're close enough that she's expecting you for Christmas.' His eyes narrowed. 'A relative, perhaps?'

She swallowed, her eyes shadowing darker as she turned from him. Like him, she'd showered after the sauna. But she hadn't bothered to dress. Instead, she wore the silk robe the chalet provided.

On any other woman, Alessio would've imagined it a form of seduction. But from the way the lapels were carefully pulled close at her throat, the belt securely cinched at her waist; from the way one hand hovered close to her thighs to keep the robe from parting, he sensed it was more of a covering than anything else.

Just as the feather boa had been? Or the multiple layers she wore that didn't make sense? From moment to moment, it was almost as if she were a different woman, with interchanging personalities.

For instance, the Gigi he'd encountered a few months back wouldn't be in such an emotional upheaval over something like this.

Which, considering he liked to distance himself from such a show of emotion, was a thing for him to be lauding her for. Instead, he was at once intrigued and irritated. Because, damn it, he *wanted* to know which one was genuine.

Diu, was he going out of his mind?

So what if everything he'd believed about Gigi Parker had been turned upside down? Perhaps under normal circumstances he would've been vexed that she'd kept an astonishing amount of intelligence hidden beneath that vacuous façade and hedonistic lifestyle.

But…he was enjoying this version of Gigi. Perhaps a little too much. And whereas with any other woman he would've quickly distanced himself, he only wanted to know more about her disagreements with the person on the other end of the phone.

His hand shot out to stay her, then he went one better and slid his fingers into her hair, massaging the knotted tension in her nape as he peered down at her.

'What are you doing?' she demanded in genuine surprise, as if she found his gentle caress strange.

'You're distressed,' he responded, in that moment unwilling to probe just why her distress fed his unnerved state. 'Tell me why.'

'Wouldn't you be if your mother called you a disappointment?' she shot out, then her face immediately closed with a touch of dismay.

Alessio wanted to pull her into his arms, to offer her comfort. But he was already unsettled by his knee-jerk reaction. He wasn't ready to compound it.

And wasn't that the most infernal thing?

He slotted away the titbit of her referring to her mother by her first name and asked the more pressing question. 'On what does she base that accusation?'

Her lips parted, then clamped shut. 'I don't think you can—'

'We're past using our current circumstances as an excuse. No one besides my flesh and blood know what I told you about my father. I'm not even sure why I told you something extremely personal, *duci*. It would make me feel a lot better if you shared in return,' he interrupted, his voice thick with emotion he was unwilling to name.

Her eyes widened. Then she licked her bottom lip.

Alessio suspected she didn't even realise she was performing that nervous tic. *A tic she didn't have before.*

He frowned, his senses prodding him hard once more. But her lips were parting, and, because he craved further insight into this woman, he once again ignored the sensation.

She raised her gaze and for the next age her eyes caught his. Held and held. Until something sharp and demanding tightened in his chest. Then spiderwebbed throughout his body, unfurling agitation and need until Alessio couldn't remember whether he was breathing in or out. Whether his preference was to drown in her eyes or die between her thighs.

Her sudden laughter drew another inward frown.

The sound was off. Fake.

'It's really not a big deal.'

His fingers dug a little deeper into her tense muscles and his senses leapt with pleasure and satisfaction when she leaned into him. 'Your obvious distress tells a different story.'

Delicate eyelids descended but before he could ask her to look at him, she raised them again. 'I think you heard most of what it was all about. She's been disappointed in my life choices for as long as I can remember. Everything I do seems…to rub her the wrong way. Including the fact that I might be stuck in another country for the holidays. She's not thrilled about the fact that I'm breaking with tradition.'

Again Alessio sensed she was withholding something, not giving him the whole picture, and while it frustrated him at least she'd answered. 'You spend every Christmas with her?'

She nodded. 'Although we spend it locked in one disagreement or the other. I've stopped trying to work out why she wants me around when it's obvious we don't get along.'

'Then maybe you shouldn't. Just accept that some families thrive on heightened emotions and decide whether that's the way you want it to be with yours.'

She blinked at him. 'Even though it makes us both emotionally dysfunctional?'

'The ideal of a perfect family is a myth, *duci*. Consider whether, if you did everything she wanted, you would find fulfilment within yourself without feeling like you've sold out.'

Shadows appeared again. 'I probably would,' she murmured. 'But I'd like to think there's a world where we can strike a balance between the two.'

He tucked his thumbs beneath her chin and tilted her face up to his. The powerful urge to kiss her distress away struck again. He barely managed to suppress the need. 'You already know where the balance is. You're distressed because *she* doesn't accept it. But I'm also thinking you might be relieved to be apart from her this year?'

Her nostrils fluttered as she inhaled sharply. 'I don't... I can't... I feel like a terrible person, but yes.'

'Don't punish yourself too severely. You might be surprised how withholding can focus a person's true goals. It might even push her to behave herself next Christmas.'

'And if she doesn't?'

'Then you'll have this experience of what it's like to spend your holidays without her.'

She stared at him as if she wanted to argue, but beneath his fingers Alessio felt her muscles soften, the few layers of tension leaving her body.

A second later she stiffened again. 'Did you just attempt to *fix* my mummy issues?' She laughed a little forcefully.

There was that switch again.

Alessio frowned inwardly, the prickling in his brain growing more insistent. The dichotomy that had grated at first was now insistently pointing in a direction he needed to heed.

Because it was almost as if in certain moments she was…acting. Putting on an inauthentic persona. Like… displaying overt sexuality then a curiously shy innocence? Like…curves and a voracious appetite where there used to be obsessive diet-watching? Like…looking a little lost in his wine cellar and being reluctant to drink when he'd seen her knock back several glasses of alcohol without blinking?

And even with the wine…

Alessio breathed through the gut punch as another memory slotted into place and the dominos started to fall, astonished that he managed to control himself before blurting out the demand. He was pleased for that restraint.

'Alessio?'

She was intelligent enough to sense the change in the room. Her beautiful eyes had grown wide and wary.

'It's easy to see the woods for the trees from a distance.' And as he said the words Alessio knew they were meant for him too. He was better off viewing what he suspected from a sensible distance too. He needed to be sure, to give a benefit of the doubt because…

Because if he was right…

The depth of betrayal and disappointment churning in his chest made him suck in a slow breath.

'I am curious as to why you call her Renata though,' he said, more to distract himself than anything else.

Tension seized her again but he didn't make a move to alleviate it. Not without risking giving himself away.

'She was a teenage mother. She liked it when people assumed she was an older sister rather than mother and daughter. She forbade us…um…me from calling her Mamma when I started school.'

As he watched her Alessio realised one thing. Whether or not his instincts proved right—and that *'us'* just now was painting a definitive picture that made things so much clearer—didn't minimise her pain.

Not if such a simple thing as claiming the woman who gave birth to her by her rightful label distressed the woman before him. Perhaps her emotions ran much deeper than he'd initially believed.

Deciding it was time to return to the realm of distance and neutrality, he dragged his hands off her silky-smooth nape, ignoring the mournful loss of her warm, supple skin. To allay the effect, he shoved his hands into his pockets. 'I came here for a reason,' he gritted out.

A flash of something lit her eyes before she nodded. 'What is it?'

'I managed to get through to my client. He's going ahead with your suggestion.'

Genuine delight lit up her eyes, chasing away most of the shadows. 'He is? That's fantastic!' Her eyes searched his for a moment longer. 'Does that mean I've passed the interview?'

Alessio's insides tightened with that curious mix of pride and fury. Answering 'yes' drew a line beneath their association, got her off the hook from whatever game she was playing. He wasn't ready for that yet.

His gaze slid past her to the snow-white landscape and, for the first time since his arrival at his chalet, he found he didn't quite mind the deplorable circumstances he found himself in.

'Let's not jump the gun yet. There are several stages to get through first.'

'Like what?'

His gaze returned to her. Not so wise ideas tumbling through his mind, Alessio decided to try one last theory. 'Come downstairs. We'll celebrate this win and discuss next steps.'

Now that he'd accepted the high probability that this woman *wasn't* Gigi Parker, he was noticing further irregularities that made him kick himself. For instance, she had a prepossession, a stillness that her sister—and he assumed he was looking at a twin version of the woman who stole from him—that Gigi didn't possess. Even the way she gravitated to the Christmas tree when they entered the living room, looking at it with almost childlike delight when the other would've completely ignored it.

Alessio could barely keep himself from staring at how the festive lights twinkling on the tree highlighted her smooth skin and perfect cheekbones, the full curve of her lips.

But he wasn't here to be enthralled by her beauty.

He crossed the room, deliberately walking close. Whatever she saw in his face made her inhale sharply, then pivot to examine an ornament.

'A drink? A cocktail perhaps?' he asked, watching her carefully.

She shook her head, then, catching his gaze, hesitated for a moment.

Another domino fell.

He recalled his thought that first night that she was

playing a part. He'd believed it was just to secure the job. But she'd been playing a part because she wasn't who she claimed to be.

Santa cielo. What an utter fool he'd been.

'Um… I'm good with wine, thanks. Then I need to make another call.'

A perfect opportunity. 'You left your phone upstairs. Here, use mine.' He plucked his phone from his pocket of his joggers, saw the blank space where the bars should be, and cursed.

Her eyes widened but he saw a flash of relief in the depths, shoring up his conviction. 'Don't tell me…'

'Yes, we've been cut off again. *Non importa.* We'll use the time wisely.'

Crossing to the drinks cabinet, he reached for his favourite cognac. After pouring her a glass of Merlot he brought the drinks to where she stood.

Their fingers brushed as she took hers, the expected sizzle of electricity arriving on cue. Alessio was close enough to see the pulse leap at her throat, to watch her take a sip and swallow. Despite the charged air between them, she didn't move to fill it with mindless chatter.

This woman who delivered succinct, invigorating conversation also knew the art of silence. Alessio hated how much he liked that.

Her gaze stayed on his for a moment before moving once more to the tree, her head tilting up to take it all in after she took a small sip of wine.

'What are you thinking?' Four innocuous words that shocked him to the core. Not once in his life had he asked a woman her innermost thoughts. Not once had he cared.

But he cared now, for whatever mystical reason. He *cared*. Because she'd pulled the wool over his eyes. And *not* because of the shadows ghosting over her face.

'It's Christmas in two days. I can't believe I won't be spending it with my mother and…' She stopped, blinked a few times, then dragged her fingers through her hair.

He tensed. 'Your mother and…?' he pushed, with a voice edged with emotions he didn't want to investigate.

'And whoever she's decided will form part of her festivities this year,' she responded. 'She turns it into a competition, you see. Makes her friends vie for the privilege of spending the holidays with Renata in some exotic place of her choosing.'

Alessio was certain now that, while she wasn't lying about her elaborate reply, she was holding something back. His thoughts leapt back to the report sitting in his inbox. The report he couldn't access without an internet connection.

She set the barely touched glass on the table and dragged both hands through her hair. 'Didn't mean for this to get so *deep*. Let's liven it up a bit, hmm? Maybe some music? Or I can solve another fixer problem for you?'

She whirled, then self-consciously caught the bottom of the robe when it flared to reveal a flash of her shapely leg.

Alessio set his empty glass down. 'We'll continue this in my study. There's an important report I'd like to access if the internet comes back.'

Her eyes searched his and she swallowed, attempting to hide her alarm. But then she nodded.

He motioned her forward with his hand, keeping his expression neutral.

With that fake smile still pinned in place, she fell into step with him as they exited the living room.

Alessio kept a tight grip on his emotions as they entered his study. From the corner of his eye, he watched her fuss with her belt, her gaze darting around the room. 'Actually, do you mind if we pick this up later?'

'Why?'

She stiffened, then immediately attempted to relax her body. 'What do you mean why?'

'You seem nervous. Why is that?' he pushed.

She shrugged. 'It's been a long and unusually…revelatory day. I think I need a little peace and quiet to process it all.'

It was close enough to the truth for Alessio to marvel how many times she'd given just enough without going all the way. Without doubt, the incident in the sauna after their kiss had been one of them. He didn't know whether to be angered or impressed at her cunning.

How ironic that she was exactly the sort of person he would pay a high premium to employ in a heartbeat. 'Is that all?'

Wide grey eyes blinked at him. 'What else could it be?'

He ventured closer, watched her throat move in another swallow. 'You wouldn't be running away from something else, would you?'

Did her breath catch? 'Like wh—?'

He reached for her, all sense leaving his brain as neutrality vanished. Even as he sealed his lips to hers, he cursed the sensation…the emotions he'd condemned for so long. Without it, he knew he wouldn't be feeling this charged *betrayal*. This potent *need*.

He would've seen this coming a mile off. He most definitely wouldn't have swallowed her husky moan as if it were manna itself, wouldn't have craved more of it as he nudged her back against the closed door and plastered his body to hers.

Santa cielo, she was so soft. So addictive!

Before he could compute the wisdom of it, he wrapped an arm around her trim waist and lifted her off her feet. Pinning her delicious body to his, he stumbled towards the wall.

'Alessio…'

Sense would've been restored if she'd pushed him away. But even as his name trembled from her delicious, duplicitous mouth, her fingers were digging into his nape, her eyes pools of pure temptation as she held onto him. As her legs parted and wrapped around his waist.

And while he was a strong-willed, ruthless man, there were some brands of temptation, he was discovering, that dissolved his control. *'Se…se…'*

They tangled in a frenzy of limbs, his hands already pulling her robe loose before roving her supple form, reacquainting himself with everything she'd denied him when she'd walked away from him at the sauna. Her breath gushed in his ear as he trailed his lips from the corner of her mouth and down her jaw and throat. As he lapped at the wild pulse beating there.

As he charted a path lower to the pebbled peak of one plump breast, groaning deep as he finally, *finally* captured the erogenous morsel. Her back arched, and his senses lit on fire.

One more taste, just *one more* and he'd…he'd…

'Oh, God…' Her gasped delight pushed him deeper into quicksand.

Diu mio. 'Gi—' He stopped short of uttering the name he knew wasn't hers.

Just as she stiffened. Then tried to scramble away from him. 'Stop.'

Alessio froze, ice drip-drip-dripping into the flames of his ardour, dousing them enough for him to refocus. To regain a crumb of control.

And remember. 'Why, *duci*?' he forced the drawl as he dragged himself away from her, watched the woman whose guilt was written all over her face. 'Because you're not Gigi Parker? Because you've been lying through your beautiful teeth since we set eyes on each other?'

A look of horror overcame her face, followed swiftly by alarm.

Alessio saw the wheels turning as her eyes darted away from his. Luckily for her, she gave up the ruse with a swift inhale.

'How did you know?' Her voice was a husky, shaky mess she couldn't control, and the sound of it aroused Alessio even further. Evidently, there wasn't a single thing about her that didn't turn him on. At least, now he unequivocally understood why.

She was not Gigi Parker.

Remarkably, now it was confirmed, he was remembering even more differences. The occasional bouts of shyness, the way she blushed at the oddest times. His nostrils flared involuntarily, taking in more of her heady scent as he stared down at her.

'I suspected. You just confirmed it.' When her eyes flared again, he continued, 'Among other things, the woman I met a few months ago existed solely on shots and cocktails. You drink wine and not very much of it. You also pretend to love the limelight when in fact I suspect you hate it.'

The deep relish in his tone had her snatching the loosened ties of her silk robe to hide herself.

He grieved the covering of her sublime body but hardened his tone. 'A little late for that, don't you think?'

'You can't expect me to still…'

'What? Give into your desires the way you've been fighting all week?'

She paled a little, which only served to highlight the deep rouge of her well-kissed lips. 'Why didn't you say something?'

He shrugged, the pressure in his groin warring with the curious chafing in his chest. He wasn't coming down with something, was he? No. He never got sick. This must be some new adverse reaction of subterfuge. One that didn't just start and end in rage. Alessio wasn't sure whether to be thankful or resentful of the sensation he couldn't totally figure out.

Enough.

'Maybe I was biding my time, seeing how far you would take it. And you were prepared to go all the way, weren't you?'

Her face flamed and he smothered a groan. Even now, with bare-faced evidence of her duplicity exposed, he found her far too alluring. A tiniest sliver of him wished he'd kept his mouth shut.

A flash of something close to hurt crossed her face before she smoothed it out. 'I'd do anything to keep my family safe.'

The prongs of accusation in her response flattened his arousal. 'Do I hear judgement in your tone, *duci*?'

Incredulously, she waved him away as if he were a pesky fly.

Swallowing a growl, he countered it by approaching her, catching her shoulders within his grasp. 'This is the part where most people show remorse. It would be great if I didn't have to drag answers out of you.'

'Would it do any good? Only I get the feeling I'd be wasting my time.'

He dragged her closer, his senses unwilling to stand the small distance between them. 'Try it and see.'

She stared at him for an age before her gaze dropped. To his mouth. Alessio stifled another groan. But again, she wiped the hazy look within seconds and had he not been watching her, he would've thought he imagined it. Unlike her sister, she was better at caging her emotions.

Much like him.

Instead of the kindred feeling he expected, Alessio grew even more disgruntled. He told himself it was because he would have to work harder at exposing her weaknesses, but it didn't quite ring true. What did ring true was the smouldering need to know her thoughts. Her feelings.

Where they went from here.

This enforced stay must be wreaking havoc on his psyche. He'd actively discouraged his previous partners from expressing anything but their willing enthusiasm for sex. Dirty talk in bed was the only form of extra-curricular discourse he welcomed. And yet now...

He dropped her shoulders and turned away. Once again, he was losing sight of his priorities. Now she'd admitted her lies, several questions needed addressing. Instead of thinking with his shaft, he needed to get to the bottom of just how he'd fallen for this subterfuge.

'We'll address everything, including this—' he waved his fingers between them '—in due course. First, tell me your real name.'

Her eyes snapped with defiance and alarm, but he spotted something else. Relief? 'It's Giada. Dr Giada Parker,' she stated with pride.

Reluctant admiration unwound inside him. Of course, she possessed a doctorate. It took a special woman to pull the wool over his eyes for this long. 'So when you said your mother was disappointed in you it obviously wasn't for what I thought. So...?'

Her relief receded a touch to be replaced by some more shadows. He knew his question drilled into the heart of the fraught relationship she had with her mother. 'She mocked me for wanting a career. Then for going further to gain a PhD.'

He lifted an eyebrow, the question clear.

'I have a doctorate in marine biology, a career my mother thought was a waste of my life.'

Surprise mingled with all the teeming emotions. 'I admit you've stunned me, Dr Parker.'

Despite the tension whipping between them, a smile teased her lips. When she blushed, the storm of hunger raging through him intensified.

'It's a bit of a relief to be called that again.'

Alessio inhaled slowly, absorbing her name, her essence. His eyes raked her face, lingering longest on her lips from where her real identity had just tumbled. 'Giada.' He breathed it.

Diu, it felt good to speak her name. And as he repeated it mentally, he was even more irritated to realise he much preferred it to the more jarring *Gigi*.

Giada.

Her sharp inhale fluttered her nostrils. Alessio realised he'd spoken her name again, infused it with something of what he was feeling. He brazened his way through it, allowing a sardonic smile to curve his lips.

'Yes, I should punish you for letting me call you by another woman's name for this long. Your twin, I presume?'

At her nod, he leaned closer, frowning when she retreated a step. Then he was smiling again because she'd caught herself, that regal chin elevating to spear him with a glare.

Colour washed into her face, even as she shook her head. 'You seem to get off on punishing people. First with my sister, and now with—'

'Don't you dare flip this on me,' he snapped, his humour vanishing. 'I punish people who cross me. And in your case it would be the most delectable way possible. A way that is making your cheeks heat up right now just thinking about it. You can be outraged all you want but you can't deny your body language.'

She opened her mouth to protest, but he quickly interrupted. 'Now, tell me where your sister is. And I advise you to come completely clean. For both your sakes.'

* * *

Emotions cascaded through Giada as Alessio stared down at her.

Primarily, it was relief. Followed by shame that she'd let her sister down. Even though the relief would be short-lived, she let it loose through her limbs, welcoming the clichéd truth setting her free as she breathed easy for the first time in almost a week.

She would deal with what that meant when she caught her breath and could find a moment to think.

But right now, heat pummelled her, making her intensely aware of every needy cell in her body. Need she desperately suppressed so she could answer his question. Alongside that need though was a feeling of almost…shock. What she'd done…almost done with him was…

She shook her head, her senses still a jumbled mess. 'Right at this minute? I don't know,' she said in answer to his question.

Alessio's eyes narrowed, the passionate man of minutes ago, not completely gone, but retreating in favour of the formidable opponent intent on bending her to his will. *And, oh, how she longed to bend*.

At least now, she could bend knowing he wouldn't address her by her sister's—God, what was wrong with her?

His hands slid beneath her shoulder blades, up her nape and spiked into her hair, while her blood dance giddily in her veins. And when the fiery blush burned its way up her face, she wanted to die a thousand deaths, especially when those very flames seem to flare in Alessio's eyes.

'Are you ready to bloom, *duci*?' he rasped, his gaze scouring her face to settle firmly on her mouth.

'Most definitely not,' she retorted hotly, even as her nipples peaked harder, her thighs twitching with need.

'Then I suggest you come up with a more satisfactory answer, *duci*.'

Or what? she wanted to taunt, to test him, see how effectively, or not, he could hang onto that iron control. Because from the way he was breathing, from the way the need prowling through her was mirrored in his eyes, his control was on a knife-edge. As was hers.

Giada would never be able to explain how she bit back the words, how she managed to breathe through the insistent urges until they eased.

'It's true. I've received just one text since we arrived.'

'What did it say?' he demanded.

The words flashed through Giada's brain.

Still no dice. Might not make it home for Xmas. You need to stall for longer. G x

Her frantic calls to Gigi's phone had gone straight to voicemail, which was why she'd called Renata. Giada hadn't even got round to asking her mother if she knew Gigi's whereabouts before Renata laid into her.

The all too familiar ripple of despair and helpless pain sheared off a trace of her awareness of Alessio. Which helped her take a step back as his hand rose. He still managed to caress her cheek, but the moment his fingers moved towards her jaw, she forced another step back.

The comfort he'd offered earlier had been far too

welcome. Even now, she yearned for more of it. Yearned to step into the warmth of his arms and let the power of her mother's censure and disappointment bounce off her. But that way lay danger and recklessness.

She'd withstood her mother's harsh and callous views of her firstborn daughter. She would power through without help from the dynamic man whose words soothed but whose eyes promised danger.

'She asked me to stall for a little longer,' she blurted, unwilling to perpetuate further lies now the truth was out. Now she was free…

To what? Dive headlong into temptation?

Something close to disappointment and, puzzlingly, vindication, snapped in his eyes, as if she'd handed him confirmation of something on a silver platter. 'So when you gave me your word on our first night here that my property would be returned to me, you were doing so on a wing and a prayer? With no knowledge at all that you'd be able to deliver?' he condemned. But behind the condemnation, there was a bleakness and resignation that stuck sharp darts into her chest.

She swallowed. Almost of their own volition, her hands rose to his shoulders. He tensed at her touch, his eyes boring lasers into hers. 'I meant it. I'll make sure it's returned to you.'

For an age he didn't reply, just appraised her with eyes that spoke their own story. Disbelief. Rage. Desire. Formidable judgement. A promise of retribution. And finally, his gaze leaving her to drop down her body…a deep, dark resolution that sent a pulse of exhilaration through her.

Slowly, his head dropped, inch by excruciating inch.

Until the tip of his nose brushed hers. His eyes didn't waver from her.

'Listen well, Giada, as I make my promise to you. You will not leave my sight until what is mine is back in my possession. And even then, I reserve the right to hold you captive until I'm satisfied that you pose no nuisance to me or my goals.'

Absurd hurt lanced through her middle.

'Get away from me,' she managed, despite her body's screaming desire to remain exactly where she was, beneath this man's powerful will and blatant, furious desire.

'Are you sure that's what you want?' he mocked, his lips twitching when her treacherous hips moved of their own accord, straining towards him.

'Yes,' she squeezed out after a long, desperate inhale. 'I may be deplorable in your eyes but even I draw the line at sleeping with a man who intends to keep me prisoner.'

'Even though you strolled into my cage with your eyes wide open?' he drawled, his scent wrapping tighter around her.

'That's the difference between you and me, I guess. I'll do anything for my family, including walking into cages, yes.'

The heat in his eyes cooled but he remained where he was. 'You deem yourself better than me?' he rasped.

'I'm not the one tossing out threats and ultimatums. My sister made a mistake by acting on impulse, and I'm sorry for that. Can you not—?'

The plea dried up when he hauled himself away from her.

She watched, eyes wide, as he dragged impatient fingers through his hair, seeking that control they'd hungrily chipped away. Sleek, beautiful muscles rippled as he inhaled and exhaled to regain it.

Deeply mesmerised, she could only watch him, her heart hammering in her throat as she leaned against the wall. Her breath caught when he pivoted to face her, his face a thunderous cloud of censure.

'Shall I tell you what that item your sister petulantly helped herself to means to me? To my family?'

Giada stumbled forward, her legs almost too weak to keep her upright. Reaching the sofa, she perched on it, tucking her legs beneath her as he prowled the room. 'Please,' she invited softly, instinct warning that whatever he intended to divulge wasn't to be taken frivolously.

His narrowed eyes examined her, determining if she was worthy of this evidently sacred piece of himself. Without preamble, he spoke.

'I told you my father paid the ultimate price. What I didn't say was that he was killed specifically because of that heirloom.'

CHAPTER EIGHT

GIADA'S JAW DROPPED, her insides twisting with sorrow and sympathy for him, and fresh anger at Gigi for putting him through this. 'I… Oh, God, I'm so sorry.'

The bleakness she'd caught glimpses of arrived and this time it stayed, dulling his eyes and tightening his jaw. It didn't diminish him one iota though. His proud bearing grew impossibly prouder, her condolences bouncing off him as he continued pacing.

It took a moment to realise he was lost in thought, probably in the past he'd just revealed.

She cleared her throat, her body swaying closer of its own volition. Closer to him. 'How…what exactly happened?' she pressed softly.

A muscle ticced in his jaw and for the longest time, she thought he'd ignore her.

Then he shook his head. 'I've often wondered if it was hubris, blind hope or just plain naïveté.' His mouth twisted but even that motion didn't detract from her absorption in him. 'Maybe it was a combination of the three,' he mused harshly.

Gathering the robe around her, Giada stayed quiet. She understood the need to work through his thoughts at a time like this. She'd needed to do the same after every confrontation with her mother.

'The Montaldis have held a certain position throughout our history. One of leadership regardless of personal desires or what the world thought we should be.'

She frowned. 'Which was what exactly?'

That twist of his lips again. 'I come from a long line of fixers, *duci mia*. One of my grandmothers many times removed was a powerhouse rumoured to be utterly indispensable to one of the popes. She birthed the legacy I've sworn to uphold.'

She didn't doubt him. 'And with that sort of power and legacy come enemies.'

His smile dimmed, still a harshly beautiful thing despite his haunted eyes and dangerous subject. '*Se*. Over the years, there have been challenges, regardless of whether or not some of the new generation just wanted a thriving family and to leave behind a legacy they're proud of.'

'Are you one of them? I'm finding that hard to believe since you're happily unattached and are swimming in the deep end of the dating pool, according to the tabloids.' Why saying that left a trail of acid in her throat, Giada refused to dissect.

She had no rights where he was concerned. None at all.

Nor did she want them.

Ignoring the void that insistence left behind, she focused as he paced towards her.

'My marital status doesn't change the fact that I'm a Montaldi. And that I'm duty-bound to right the wrongs done to a father who may have been overly optimistic in his thinking that he could change the course of tradition, but who still didn't need to give his life for instigating that change.' The thick, unshakeable vow fell like an anvil in the room from a man who would not be swayed from his destiny.

Giada didn't even need to voice the questions brimming on her tongue. She only needed to remain silent so he could spell out how very wrong Gigi had been in crossing him.

'My father was determined to steer the responsibilities of his birthright in a new direction, rather for just the wealthy and privileged—helping fix wrongs for those who deserved it. Those with integrity who would pay it forward so others benefitted. He studied to be a lawyer and he was exceptional at it. He was exemplary at being a fixer. I learned everything I know from him.'

'But not everyone agreed with the new path?' she guessed.

He exhaled deep and long. Then his lips twisted. 'No. The inevitable crooked politicians and underworld drug lords cropped up with alarming frequency. They wanted to use his services. But he wouldn't be swayed. He ignored all the warnings because he believed he was doing the right thing. And when he told me, I… feared for him.'

'But you were still proud of him,' she slid in, the note throbbing in his voice evident.

He looked startled for a minute, then he gave a single nod. '*Se*. Power needn't always come from being feared. He taught me that too as a boy.'

And in those words, Giada made a discovery.

It was both startling and alarming.

Because its effect on her left her frantically out of breath and on edge.

Alessio wasn't a man who sold his services to the highest bidder without qualms. Every client he'd taken on had something fundamentally personal at stake. Something, if lost, money wouldn't replace.

Underneath his ruthless, brooding exterior, the man she was snowed in with possessed an unyielding core of integrity.

And the reason she was so aflame at that discovery?

It ramped up the unstoppable appeal that seemed to grow and expand and seethe with hunger with every second she spent in his company.

'You looked up to him,' she added softly.

Again he looked mildly nonplussed, and, even though he didn't nod, the flash of pain in his eyes spoke volumes. 'He was a great father. He cared for his family and his integrity and honour never wavered regardless of the pressure from others on how he should lead the Montaldi family.'

'What did the crest have to do with it?' she asked when the silence stretched.

'In Montaldi tradition, the person who possesses it has the right to challenge the ruling family for leadership. My father believed he had nothing to worry about because our family had retained it for four generations. We were easily the largest and most influential family in Sicily. No other family had dared to challenge a Montaldi in over ninety years.' He paused, his eyes growing bitter and bleaker with harrowing memories.

'But he didn't account for the betrayal coming from within his own family.'

Her gasp echoed in the chilling silence of the room. 'Who?'

The haunted darkness intensified, and within it Giada saw the ruthless man forged from loss, betrayal and determination. A man who plainly and unequivocally meant to avenge his father. A man who would strike down anyone who stood in his way.

A man who would go to the ends of the earth to reclaim the very tool he needed to achieve that goal.

The bracing shudder that rushed over her brought blinding enlightenment. She barely managed to squeeze her eyes shut and moan in despair as the true repercussions of what Gigi had done slammed home.

She wanted to throw herself at his feet in that moment. To beg for whatever sliver of mercy resided in his heart. But he was speaking again, and in that nanosecond she realised she couldn't. They were stuck here for another handful of days at the minimum, a week if they weren't lucky.

Divulging that Gigi currently had no clue where the Montaldi family crest was would be like sealing herself in with a predator and hoping it wouldn't devour her out of sheer fury and frustration.

'My father had three younger brothers. They didn't like the new direction he wanted to adopt; they preferred to sell our services to the highest bidder. When he wouldn't be swayed, they took over...by force. They gunned him down in front of his wife and sons on a Sunday after attending mass and praying by his side. My mother went from being a beloved matriarch to being cast aside like yesterday's garbage, thrown out of her home with her sons. She went from donating large tracts of her time and money to charities to not being even worthy of charity herself because she'd been black-listed by my uncles. We were forced to leave Sicily, to live in halfway houses across the country while she worked menial jobs. She died heartbroken and broken. But with her last breath, she asked me to make things right. So you see, Giada, reclaiming my possession isn't a trivial matter to me.'

That momentary urge to disclose the whole truth was smothered beneath the need to assuage the obvious hell of his confession.

It grew and grew until she couldn't hold still. Couldn't watch him suffer from across the cold distance between them. Before she thought better of it, Giada rose off the sofa and approached him.

'Yes, I see, Alessio. I see it clearly,' she murmured.

He watched her with eyes that didn't really focus on her, lost as he was in his tortured memories. The yearning to erase them drew her hands up, extended to him.

And when he didn't move away or reject her, she touched the backs of his strong hands with hers. The skin-to-skin contact was raw and visceral enough to draw a hiss from him. To make *her* gasp low and needy, every inch of her flesh straining for more.

She dragged her hands higher, up and over his wrists and forearms, then higher still to his elbows. Then she changed direction, running her touch beneath his polo shirt and over his lower abs.

Packed muscles jumped beneath her hands, his eyes turning molten gold as he continued to watch her every move with avid eyes, his breathing truncating as she explored his tight six-pack.

'Be careful what you're doing, Giada.'

The sound of her name sent another bolt of desire through her, making her so thankful that she could now shed her false persona. That she could be who she was with him. Her hands drifted up, over his flat nipples. He hissed in another breath, his eyes growing even more hooded.

'Giada…' There was thick warning and barely leashed arousal in that single word, making her moan.

'You moan when I say your name. You like it, don't you?'

The rough arousal in his voice lit a fuse to hers, and the confession tumbled out before she could stop it. 'She may be my identical twin so I should be used to it but… I don't like being called by another woman's name.'

'I hardly called you Gigi anyway. Perhaps deep down I knew,' he rasped. 'Perhaps I should've analysed why I walked into that club certain I would be handing you over to the authorities immediately, but then…decided against it. Why watching you blush and try to hide your body from me made my senses tingle in warning that something wasn't right but I didn't really want to explore it anyway.'

It was the height of foolishness to attribute anything beyond simple intuitiveness to it, but something leapt within her, a revelry in his statement that made her sway closer, her senses alight with need. 'Whatever it is, I'm glad you didn't.'

His nostrils flared, her open confession seeming to affect him. He started to reach for her but then froze.

'Before we go any further, I need to know. Is there someone in Dr Parker's life besides your mother and sister who will give you grief for your absence?' The question was rasped with a displeased bite that sent a shiver through her.

Her heart lurched, then thumped hard in her chest. 'Are you asking me if I'm attached, Alessio?'

Perhaps it was the unwittingly husky way she uttered his name that made his breath expel in that rapid way. Or it was all in her mind.

'*Se*. I am. Because I don't have qualms about stating unequivocally that I don't share,' he warned. 'That I'm extremely possessive in the things I crave enough to keep.'

Her heart lurched now for a different reason, yearnings she was desperately unwise to harbour, surging high with what it'd look like if Alessio Montaldi craved her. Fought to *keep* her. But that would never happen because, even now, the clock ticked down to their eventual separation.

But until then, she wanted…no, needed this moment. And she intended to take it. And once again, it was so very freeing to speak her truth. 'You don't need to worry about attachments. Possess away,' she invited boldly.

Within one breath and the next, he caught her to him, plastering her against the warmth of his body. 'This unrestrained side of you… I like it. I much prefer it to the pretence from before.'

Another moan slipped out, her hands stealing around his neck so she could strain herself closer to his hot body. So she could alleviate the hunger ripping her to pieces.

'I want more of it,' he demanded thickly. 'And you can start by telling me that you want me.'

'You have eyes and a brilliant mind, Alessio. You don't need confirmation.'

'Maybe not, but a man likes to hear that the prickly woman he's going slowly mad over is finally yielding to him.'

Her gasp echoed between their lips, the quirk of his eyebrow conveying that he enjoyed the effect of his words on her, that he was anticipating her giving him exactly what he wanted. And like a snake dancing to the tune of a hypnotist, she lost herself to everything about Alessio Montaldi as he swung her up in his arms, exited his study and hurried them upstairs.

In his bedroom, he stopped at the edge of the bed with one eyebrow raised in heated demand, awaiting the answer she'd yet to give.

'I want you, Alessio. Very much. Maybe *too* much.'

With drool-worthy smoothness, he divested himself of his polo shirt and designer joggers. Then he swooped down, stopping at the last minute so the brush of his lips over hers was a mere whisper. 'There's no such thing as too much when it comes to this.'

This entailed a caress on her waist, a trail of fire up her ribcage before his hands closed possessively over her breasts, moulding with a deep groan as his lips completed the journey, sealing over hers in a forceful play of lust that had her senses diving into free fall.

The dizzying pairing of his thumbs tormenting her nipples and his tongue delving between her lips to dance with hers weighted her limbs with desire. The sheer power of it was so astonishing and bright and new that she barely felt it when he nudged her one final time to fall onto the bed.

He followed, his body barely parting from hers, the move so smooth and seamless, she felt a momentary twinge at how expert he was at this.

Then she set the troubling thought free. It had no room here.

This moment was all about seizing transient pleasure. More, it was about offering herself as a balm and barrier to the tormenting memories their conversation had unearthed.

If the journey also delivered mind-numbing pleasure along the way, the kind she suspected her brief and unsatisfactory forays into her two previous relationships hadn't managed to achieve…well, then who was she to look a sublime gift horse in the mouth?

The thought settled deep, producing a smile and a punch of pleasure as she moaned and arched into his touch.

He lifted his head, stared down at her, his eyes aglow with desire. 'You smile like a siren of old and display this breathtaking body so delightfully, I'm almost daunted by the prospect of being a slave to your wiles.'

'Almost? Meaning you think you're immune to it?' she asked, a substantial part of her frozen in anticipation of his answer.

'*Se*. Because base emotion, no matter how divine and powerful, is transient. We can stoke it all we want, but there's a beginning and an end. Then we have no choice but to put the past where it belongs and move on.'

A pang seared her. Telling herself she shouldn't take it to heart, that he was referring to their discussion of his father and his own avenging role, his words, didn't work. It drilled into a soft and vulnerable place within her, warning her to take him seriously...or else.

But, his warning delivered, Alessio was sliding one strong arm beneath her, accepting the offering she'd foolishly made moments ago, and bringing her even closer against him until they were plastered from chest to thigh, until his powerful legs tangled with hers and the thick imprint of his erection left no doubt as to what was about to occur.

What she'd moaned and craved only a minute ago.

She still wanted it. She'd be a hypocrite to deny it. But perhaps he'd done her a favour by killing any thoughts of this being more than a physical exchange of pleasure. That she, with weighty family baggage of her own, could somehow help him carry his.

'I'm losing you,' he rasped with a heavy hint of displeasure.

Do you care? she wanted to throw back. She held her tongue. Asking that suggested she wanted a deeper insight into and a connection with a man who had laid his cards on the table.

So she shook her head and spiked her fingers into his hair. Summoning another smile, she slicked her tongue over her lips, more out of hunger than a need to titivate.

That it drew a ravenous growl from deep within him was neither here nor there.

He wanted her.

She wanted him.

It only needed to be as simple as that.

And when he lowered his head and recaptured her mouth, his body pressing her deeper into the bed, while swiftly divesting her of her robe, Giada finally set her roiling thoughts aside and succumbed to his mastery.

Alessio couldn't stop the emotional claws from digging deeper into him.

And no, it didn't help that his brain mockingly reminded him that he'd thrown this door wide open himself. A door he hadn't opened in so long that he'd believed it'd rusted shut for ever.

Diu mio, he'd told her about his father.

About the uncles who, even at this moment, were squabbling among themselves while warily scheming about how to deal with their powerful, intensely vengeful nephew.

Most sacred of all, he'd told her about his mother.

It was as if the moment he'd turned on the tap, he couldn't shut it off. And then she'd further scrambled his brain with her giving touch.

While it'd turned lustful very quickly, Alessio knew it hadn't started out that way. She'd offered simple comfort, his stark words of loss and pain touching her enough for her to reach out. To display emotion he'd been utterly defenceless against.

But he'd salvaged the situation…hadn't he?

She moved beneath him, and he angled his focus to the stunning woman offering herself so willingly to him.

Yes, he had.

Hell, he'd gone one better and shattered any misplaced notions she held towards what this meant. Which meant everything was fine.

There would be no messy emotional fallout when this unstoppable chemistry ran its course.

He was safe.

Alessio repeated those three words to himself on a loop as eager fingers dug into him, his mouth trailing her silky-smooth skin, dragging sounds from her that lit up the erotic flames in his blood.

He was safe.

So he tasted her, licked his way down to the tight rose peak of her plump breast and helped himself to her decadent flesh. Groaned deep when her back arched, willing him on as he suckled and grazed, his fingers working down her belly to the delightful heat between her legs.

At her lust-saturated cry, he turned his attention to her other peak, delivered the same strokes of pleasure as he explored her feminine core. He slid one finger, then two inside her tight heat, thrusting in rhythm to her rolling hips.

'Oh, God, that feels so good,' she moaned.

He raised his head, eager to see her pleasure for himself, devour her open, passion-drenched features. '*Se*, and it will get even better,' he vowed throatily.

Because he needed to make her forget what came before. Needed to dwell on nothing else but the sublime bliss to wash away the vulnerable exposure that haunted him.

He groaned in satisfaction and a little wonder at how thrillingly responsive she was when she met his gaze and gasped, 'Yes, *please*.'

A different sort of recklessness overcame him, one that insisted he give her everything she desired, turn himself inside out to leave his indelible mark on this woman his subconscious had known much sooner than he had.

So he returned to his ministrations with renewed vigour and was rewarded with her deeper cries, the mesmeric sight of her chasing release only *he* could provide. And even as she fell into her first, mindless climax, Alessio was hungry for more, for a deeper connection that had him reaching for the condom and ripping it open with his teeth.

The tremors that seized his hands as he drew the latex down his length, he attributed to hunger. It could be nothing else. He wouldn't permit it.

But it seemed his little siren wasn't a passive participant.

She rose onto her elbows when he slid between her thighs, her gaze darting between his face and where he was poised at the heart of her.

'You like watching me possess you, Dr Parker?' he breathed against her lips.

A deep blush rushed up her neck, and, since he didn't have to hold himself back any more, he licked its path to her cheek, then the corner of her mouth, before, with a groan seeming to burst from his very soul, he fused his mouth to hers and thrust into her slick heat.

Her hoarse cry of pleasure was almost his undoing, her tight welcoming making him clench his jaw to hold onto control.

At the roll of her hips, Alessio let out a shout before the very devil took possession of him. Capturing her arms above her head, he drew back and thrust deeper, harder, a desperation to the joining that struck a sliver of fear through his heart.

Because it'd never been like this with any woman before Giada.

And with the depth of hunger still prowling through him, he feared the spell would only get stronger.

And he might not have a choice but to do something about it. Because his path couldn't change. Not when he was so close to righting the past's wrongs.

He took her like a man possessed.

And Giada loved every second of it, revelled in the sweat that engulfed them both, delighted in his harsh breaths and guttural Sicilian words he showered over her. Then his beastly roar as he found his own release.

Did it absolutely terrify her just how much she relished his touch? Oh, yes. But would she have stopped it if her very life depended on it?

No.

That realisation thumped its ominous beat inside her long after their gasping breaths had calmed and their racing hearts had decelerated. Long after the man who'd taken her with such magnificent mastery had drifted into heavy sleep, the thick band of his arm curled around her to keep her close to him.

And even as she called herself ten kinds of fool for succumbing to his captivating masculinity, another tsunami of longing was threatening to sweep her under, so strong, so powerful that she had to bite down on her lip to keep from moaning her need and despair.

Was this the type of heady sensations her sister and mother had been chasing for as long as she could remember?

Was this a warning glimpse of what this could turn into if she didn't put her guard back up and fast? This hedonistic sensation that only more of Alessio would assuage?

If it was then…perhaps she owed them an apology.

Owed them understanding. Because the very thought of being under this potent spell for a day longer, never mind how many days she was trapped in this glorious chalet, was terrifying.

And alarmingly exhilarating.

But…didn't she know how to survive sustained threats?

Yes, she did. How many times had she butted heads with her mother and held her ground? How many times had she withstood Gigi's mockery and walked away with the burning belief that she was doing what was right for *her*? So what if Alessio's brand of temptation was unlike anything she'd felt before?

She'd withstood the harsh and frozen wilderness of Antarctica.

She would survive cutting herself completely off from this too.

She must.

Resolution burning within her, Giada sucked in a sustaining breath and slid from the bed. Then glanced back, the compulsion impossible to resist.

He remained asleep, a thick strand of hair tumbling over his forehead. His sleek bronze upper body was on full display, the sheets tangled around his lean hips.

She turned away from the masterpiece that was Alessio Montaldi, her feet weighted with lead as she caught up her dressing robe and dragged herself along the darkened hallways and back to her room. To the cold sheets that should've restored a slice of sanity but only reminded her what she'd left behind.

It didn't...*couldn't* matter.

Now she'd placed most of her cards on the table, she needed to work on extricating herself from this nightmare. Her fingers trembled as she searched for the phone she hadn't used in almost a week and turned it on, hoping against hope that there was a signal now the snow had stopped.

But fate and the tech gods weren't in a giving mood.

Tossing it aside, she determinedly slid back between the sheets and closed her eyes, fully expecting to toss and turn till daybreak. But perhaps, because she was still caught in the aftermath of a thousand emotional cyclones, sleep swiftly overcame her. Sleep crowded with dreams of writhing bodies and thick words of passion that made her cry out in pleasure only to be thwarted at the final culmination, making a complete mockery of her restfulness.

Still, she told herself she'd done the right thing as she rose and showered, donning ripped leggings before adding her bra, the see-through top she still detested, and the sweater.

Feeling exposed, she stepped out of the bedroom.

The smell of coffee drew her to the kitchen, and when that turned out to be empty, to the dining room, and the man sitting at the head of the elegant oak table, his gaze on the inch-thick document next to his coffee cup.

Giada took a moment to ground herself, to will her mind away from what had happened last night. But the curtains were open, and the light was falling on him, and she was weak enough to just...*absorb* his dynamic beauty, which transcended extraordinary good looks.

Something so uniquely him she doubted it could be replicated in this lifetime or the next, despite him being dressed in a simple pair of cashmere sweats and a black T-shirt.

Giada tried not to stare at the corded muscles that rippled beneath the fabric when he sensed her scrutiny, lifted his head and caught her gaze from across the room.

Where she'd expected cold indifference, there was narrow-eyed scrutiny that held...pained affront. He tracked her as she crossed to her seat.

A tall carafe of coffee waited and, to her surprise, the domed dish he waved her to next to his.

She lifted the lid and saw crispy bacon and scrambled eggs. On the table, a silver rack of fresh golden toast waited. 'You cooked?'

One eyebrow arched. 'You seem surprised.'

She was. Except his expressive eyes said she'd wronged him anew.

'Did you expect to survive on leftovers indefinitely?' he asked.

'Well, hopefully not indefinitely.'

Perhaps he noted her desperation as her gaze flicked to the window. Or he was just vexed with her because when she looked back, his jaw was set.

'If you're hoping to make a quick escape, you're going to be disappointed. The weather forecast predicts much of the same for the next few days, at the very least. Looks like we're definitely spending Christmas here.'

A pained sound escaped her before she could stop it.

He stiffened, eyed her with deep sardonicism. 'Was I that bad in bed?'

She gasped as her head swung towards him. His face remained an irritated mask, but something lurked in his eyes. 'I... What do you mean?'

'You look downright wretched at the thought of spending a minute more in this place whereas yesterday you'd almost accepted the situation.'

She tucked her hair behind her ear, her senses leaping and twisting just from his scent and body heat. 'You can't deny that a lot has happened since yesterday, besides the...the...'

'Sex?' he supplied in a droll tone.

A blush ate up her face and his features thawed just a tiny fraction.

She licked her lips and almost moaned at their sensitivity. 'Not necessarily. I would've thought you'd like to get out of here even more than I would.'

He shrugged. 'Not enough to risk hypothermia or worse. As frustrating as it may be, I've accepted the situation. Until I can change it, there's no point in fighting it.'

Was there a warning in there? She shook her head.

'And...not necessarily?' he drawled.

Her breath shortened at the intensity in his eyes. 'So I wasn't entirely terrible, then?'

'You don't need your ego stroked in that department, surely?' she snapped.

He took his time to answer, lifting his espresso cup and peering at her over it. His throat moved in a strong swallow, and he set it down before one corner of his mouth lifted in a quirky smile. 'No, I do not. Although you've served me a first that…intrigues.'

Her eyes widened. 'A first?'

'You're the only woman to vacate my bed before I have to encourage her out of it,' he confessed, that edge back in his tone.

'You sound more peeved than intrigued.' She forced a shrug and cut up the bacon on her plate, even though she doubted she would be able to push down a bite. 'Maybe I prefer my own company in bed after…'

Low, deep laughter rumbled from him but when she glanced up she noticed it didn't quite reach his eyes. 'What an intriguing creature you are, Dr Parker. You're deliciously passionate in bed, yet you can barely mention the word sex without turning red,' he mused.

Giada ignored the heat intensifying in her cheeks. 'It doesn't matter one way or the other. What happened last night isn't going to happen again.' The words emerged in a rush so she could hide behind them. Because up until she actually uttered them, Giada had feared she would change her mind. Feared she would succumb to temptation again.

He tensed, every trace of humour vaporising. For an age, dark gold eyes scoured her face, a muscle ticing in his jaw. 'Tell me why,' he barked.

Mild shock shivered down her spine. 'Because it was a mistake.'

'You regret it.'

She pursed her lips, the need to say yes warring with the truth she loathed to admit, which was that she was terrified of the depth of her own need. So, hoping she had one last performance in her, she raised her chin. 'Yes. It shouldn't have happened in the first place.' When explosive silence met her words, she blurted, 'I'm not in the habit of sleeping with men I barely know, or...' She stopped, unable to clearly define what Alessio was.

'Or men you're in the middle of deceiving?' he bit out.

She flinched.

He saw it and his eyes gleamed. 'At least you seem to have the semblance of a conscience.'

Furious flames ate away the last of her nerves. Setting her cutlery down, she faced him, intent on setting him straight on a few things.

'I was never without a conscience, Alessio. What I did I did out of love for my sister. It's the same way you care for your brother.'

The flames in his eyes turned livid. 'You will not compare the two.'

'Why not? Because you deem yourself much more superior to me? To Gigi? Tell me you wouldn't do anything for your brother. Aren't you right this moment in the middle of a years-long campaign to avenge your father?'

He surged to his feet. 'Watch yourself, *bedda mia*.'

Hearing the endearment snarled with fury didn't stop her memory from reliving it one more time. Before she shoved it away and stood too, her chest heaving with affront. 'Would your father want you to do what you plan to your uncles? What about your mother?'

Alessio stepped up to her, his eyes twin flames of righteous fury. 'I watched my mother struggle through life with her heart torn from her chest, the extended family she loved almost as much as she loved her husband and sons mocking her as she struggled to feed her children. Every last one of them turned their backs on her and colluded to ensure she could never rise out of the gutter they threw her in. So yes, when my mother made me swear on her deathbed that I would restore honour to the Montaldi name, I promised her I would. And nothing is going to deter me from that path. *Capisci?*'

CHAPTER NINE

IT WAS ALMOST laughable the way she'd thought this Christmas might turn out to be different just because she wasn't locked in acrimony with her mother in some exotic location.

The location was intensely breathtaking, sure.

The snow had let up at last and, with the sunlight glinting off it, it was the purest illusion designed to make one forget one's problems.

Almost.

Because even as she stared at the enthralling landscape, even as she tried to see the upside of this Christmas Eve, the *thunk-thunk-thunk* of Alessio's boxing gloves as they connected with intent on the punching bag gave ample testimony that she'd swapped one emotionally charged arena for another.

The opposing characters might be different, but the theatre was the same. Which begged the question—was there something wrong with her?

Was she destined to fight futile wars with people she let close? And yes, Alessio Montaldi had slipped beneath her guard, had imprinted himself on a vital part of her she knew wouldn't fade away easily.

Even now, after he'd warned her off voicing her opinion about his great and noble plan for avenging his parents, her heart continued to ache for him. Had ached after he'd walked off and left her in the dining room. She would've retreated and hidden away in her bedroom if that hadn't felt like a cowardly thing to do.

She'd relocated herself to the cinema room instead, attempting to distract herself with a classic Christmas movie she could barely focus on, each *thunk* making her stomach churn. Making her hate herself for her inability to shut it out and—

'I can hear you thinking from out here,' he observed from the doorway.

Giada tried not to show that he'd startled her. That every cell in her body now screamed at his proximity.

Instead, she forced a shrug. 'Then, by all means, remove yourself,' she said with tart resignation. Because as much as she wanted to brush away or bury yet another confrontation with someone else she…she cared about, the same bruising sensation arrived. Then deepened. Branding pain and despair into her soul because Alessio Montaldi signified high stakes. She'd given him her body. And, she feared, a lot more besides.

Otherwise, would she be *this* disconsolate? Would she experience this perplexing urge to stand her ground and surrender at the same time?

'I could, but I fear it would just follow me around,' he said.

And because she was weak and needy, she turned on the lounge seat she'd thrown herself on at some point she couldn't remember and stared at him as he ambled towards her.

'Would you throw some more clothes on, please?'

He didn't bother answering, only smirked as he stopped beside her, a towering display of masculinity frying a shameful number of her brain cells as he slowly unwound the protective bindings around his hands.

'Is that why you're hiding in here? Because my half-dressed state bothers you?' he taunted.

'Not at all. I'm just giving you space.'

'No, you're not. You're discontented with where I stand on certain issues and how we ended things this morning'

'You're wrong,' she countered heatedly. Because admitting it to herself was one thing, blatantly exposing her vulnerabilities was quite another.

'I propose we put that to one side. I don't wish to be locked in battle with you.' His gaze fixed hard on hers, a sincerity glowing within that made her protest wither away. Made her realise something else.

This was unlike her fights with her mother. Truce-calling never came into play with Renata. They tended to fester underneath every conversation until they eventually parted ways, then inevitably picked up where they'd left off at their next meeting. Always worse, never better.

She exhaled now, her roiling insides settling a little. *Better.* 'I don't want that either,' she confessed, much to her surprise and alarm.

He nodded, then without ceremony tossed away the binding and stretched out on the leather seat next to her.

She gasped. 'What are you doing?'

One arm propping his head, he watched her in that unnervingly intense way. 'Making up. I'm told it can lead to all sorts of delectable outcomes,' he rasped, his accent slightly thickening.

Exasperation was timely in diluting the turbulence caused by his nearness, his seeming geniality, and the furnace blazing in his eyes. 'And you wouldn't know because no woman has ever disagreed with you, of course.' Her droll tone emerged a little acerbic, fuelled by the jealousy twisting inside her.

A very masculine, very smug smile graced his lips. 'Exactly so. My past experiences have been much more agreeable. But you'll be pleased to know I find your spirit quite stimulating.'

She jerked upright, dragging her fingers through her hair that had come loose. 'Alessio, this is a—'

His fingers meshing into her hair stopped her words cold. Or perhaps it stopped it *hot*. 'This really should've been my first clue,' he rasped, his eyes following his fingers through her hair. 'It was very different a few months ago. And it has a wildness to it that is quite captivating,' he murmured throatily.

'I can alter it if you want to forget that I'm not my sister,' she said much too bitterly.

Displeasure flashed gold flames in his eyes. 'Touch it and I *will* put you over my knee and spank that delicious bottom.'

Her nostrils fluttered, a decadent thrill rushing through her that shocked her even more than his salacious words. Because that *rush* suggested she wanted him to do just that. Which was preposterous, wasn't it? She wasn't into kinky stuff...of any kind. *Yet?* 'Still threatening me with corporal punishment, I see. How primitive of you.'

His head tilted, slanting a wave of chocolate-brown hair over his forehead. 'Is it though? I'm merely warning that I'm prepared to fight for what I want.'

Sensation rushed faster through her veins, stinging her like frantic little bees. Her nipples hardened and surged against her sweater. She mourned her exposing attire blatantly announcing his effect on her. As for the heat surging into her cheeks…she shifted closer to the fire, hoping he'd attribute that to her proximity to the flames.

But one glance into his smouldering honey-gold eyes and she knew he could tell exactly how his words affected her. Hell, his lips quirked with mockery as his gaze dropped to her chest.

She lifted one shoulder, feigning calm, attempting not to feel the heavy weight of the hair he seemed obsessed with brushing down her back.

Most importantly, she didn't want to reveal how deep his words settled into her soul. 'You…you want to fight for me?'

His eyelids swept down momentarily, shielding his emotions from her. But she caught the tic at his temple, saw the way his nostrils flared. 'When the alternative is to prowl the rooms and hallways of the chalet in a sub-par mood, then yes. I'd rather we were on more agreeable terms. Or at the very least the agita was one that brings us both satisfaction.'

He meant it in a purely physical sense, of course, but it didn't stop her heart from lurching. From *yearning*. Because no one had fought for her before. Ever. All her life she'd fought for every crumb of regard or happiness.

So even if this was a temporary truce, even if they returned to disagreeing minutes or hours from now, for this moment in time she would halt the upheaval. Give into the soaring enticement and embrace the warmth that came with it.

It therefore was no task at all to sway closer, to moan when his fingers spiked into her hair and angled her face to his. To blink in impatience when all he did was hold her there, his scrutiny soul-deep.

'Alessio, please kiss me,' she gasped, something inside desperate to grasp the moment before it slipped out of her hand.

His eyes turned molten but he still withheld her wish. 'It is true that, right now, my immediate need is to bury my fingers in those lush curls, feel them come alive around my limbs and take it from there. But first, I need you to give me the true reason you didn't want this to happen again,' he breathed against her lips.

Giada's stomach dipped in alarm. She'd bared so much. As he'd said, once Gigi resurfaced with his precious heirloom, they'd never see each other again. In a matter of days, they would be memories to each other.

Past but not forgotten. I'll never forget him.

'Giada.' The rasped command was unmistakable.

She sucked in a breath, the hand that had somehow found its way to his bare chest digging into his flesh, as if he could stop the ocean of anguish from sweeping her away. 'I've striven so hard not to be anything like Renata. I know she's my mother and I shouldn't think badly of her but...'

'A part of you reciprocates the disappointment she

strives, unjustifiably, I think, to find in you? And you feel guilty for it?'

Her gasp at his concise summation drew a ghost of a smile from him. 'Yes.'

'And you think sharing my bed, and wanting to do it again, makes you like her?'

'It's not…something I've done before.' And it terrified her how addicted she could get to, not just sharing her body with him, but even this…delving-beneath-the-skin thing she was doing.

A flame of triumph lit his eyes for the briefest moment. 'I'm glad to hear it, *bedda mia*. And that in itself should tell you that there's no slippery slope unless you create one yourself.' His thumb slid back and forth over her lips, his eyes darkening at her hitched breathing. 'This might feel like it's out of your control, but ultimately the choices you make are entirely within your power and no one else's.'

Perhaps this was the reason Alessio Montaldi commanded power and turned the world's most influential men into his willing acolytes. Because just then, Giada felt like she could move mountains with her bare hands. As if the years of clashing with Renata, while heartaching, had forged her into a woman who could hold her head up and declare herself *enough*.

Tears prickled her eyelids as she opened her mouth, not entirely sure what to say to Alessio. Thank you, maybe?

But a heavy look was passing through his own eyes, a shifting in the air that said perhaps he knew what was happening to her. Was caught in it, too? A blink later, it was gone. And his head was descending.

'You will not regret this, *se*?' he rasped huskily. Insistently.

She shook her head, a glut of emotion overwhelming her.

'Say it, *tesoro*.'

'No regrets. Absolutely none.'

A thick groan erupted, then he was fusing his mouth to hers, nudging her back on the leather seat, his expert hands stripping them both.

And as he thrust hard and deep inside her, and she delivered herself up for the exhilarating ride to nirvana, Giada affirmed to herself that, no, there was no regret this time.

But there *was* possible collateral damage of her deeper emotions. Because Alessio Montaldi hadn't just woven magic on her body. He'd also claimed a part of her soul.

'Buon Natale, duci.'

Giada kept her eyes closed, but the smile that took hold of her face lit through her heart and soul. She was well burrowed into the rich cotton sheets they'd eventually pulled over themselves somewhere in the early hours, after the thrilling Christmas Eve that had included another sumptuous dinner, champagne, and an attempt to watch a Sicilian movie that had been interrupted far too frequently with seeking hands and lips, thick, sexy demands and throaty moans.

The best part of it all had been making love with

Alessio against the window of his bedroom while the snow fell outside, knowing this memory was seared in her heart for ever.

Now, with the smell of coffee teasing her nostrils and the promise of a stunning, masculine vision when she rolled over...?

Best. Christmas. Ever.

She lingered in that incredible feeling for a moment longer. Then yelped when a cascade of light objects bounced off her body. Turning over, Giada inhaled sharply as the glittering baubles rolled over the sheets.

Beside the bed, Alessio stood holding the giant white crystal-studded bag he'd evidently just emptied over her. And the contents he'd just emptied? Her eyes widened as the countless sea of ornaments danced around her. The same dark gold globes she'd seen hanging on the tree. Filled with priceless gifts.

'W-what...what's this for?' she blurted.

One eyebrow arched in wicked teasing as he tossed the empty bag aside. 'It's Christmas Day. Take a wild guess.'

'But...we can't. I mean, this isn't a normal...we're just stuck here under...certain circumstances—'

'Which we've agreed we're going to make the best of,' he said with an edge to his tone as he prowled onto the bed, sending a few of the baubles scattering. He settled over her, elbows on either side of her head as he brushed his nose with hers, then let loose a smile that stole what was left of her breath away. 'So once again, *Buon Natale,* Dr Parker,' he breathed against her lips.

Giada tried to stop the shameless melting. To stop her heart and soul from relabelling her thoughts from moments ago to Best Christmas For Ever. But she couldn't. Something fundamentally important and essential shifted inside her as she exhaled and responded, 'Merry Christmas, Alessio.'

They kissed as if they each searched for something essential in the other. As if this moment, while verbally unacknowledged, was significant. And when they parted, he stared down at her with heavy contemplation, his eyes boring into hers for answers she dared not give.

Even as he moved away towards the tray bearing coffee and breakfast things, the heaviness lingered. Two cups poured, he handed her one, then sprawled himself on the side of the bed, reaching out with his free hand to run a thumb over her lower lip for an age before he sat back.

'Open your presents,' he rasped, tossing her one orb before he lifted his cup to take a healthy sip.

Giada's fist closed around it, her insides twisting with feelings she didn't want to name. 'I don't have anything for you.'

His gaze remained long and steady on her, its focus far too probing for her liking. 'On the contrary, you've given me an alternative view of what this day could be. And I'm not altogether…unappreciative.'

'What do you mean?'

He looked a touch impatient, a touch chagrined, as if he hadn't meant to reveal that. Then he said abruptly, 'My Christmas Day is spent mostly visiting my parents' graves. It was my mother's favourite time of year. Massimo and I spend a significant portion of the day with her. It's a duty I'm honoured to perform, but it's not without its challenges.'

She couldn't pretend not to care, not to stop the swell of emotion for this man whose heart had been so devastatingly ripped from him by those who should've treasured him. The idea of him spending all Christmas Day at a cemetery or crypt with his mother felt too harrowing to conceive.

Tossing the present aside, she set the coffee down, rose and went to the edge of the bed, slid her arms around his waist. 'If you don't mind that you're stuck here with me, then I'm glad your day has been a little different.'

He exhaled sharply, then stilled, his eyes fixed on her upturned face. 'Tell me something, Dr Parker.'

She excused the madness that made her insides thrill to hear him using her doctorate. If anyone had mentioned a charismatic Sicilian man would make her feel so 'seen' she would've rolled her eyes and flaunted her feminist card. 'Yes?' she invited throatily instead.

'You've mentioned your mother a few times but not your father.'

Tension shaved off a layer of recklessness. When she tried to pull away, he held her still. Sighing, because, hell, she was in far too deep already. What was another revelation? What was opening her innermost heart and letting him see the real her, anguish, warts and all? 'That's because he's never been in the picture.'

'Meaning?'

'Meaning my mother decided when she was pregnant that she would be better off as a single parent. And my father obviously concurred because he moved to New Zealand and spurned any attempts I made to contact him when I was old enough. Call me naïve but

I thought the man who insisted his children be given his name would be interested but...' She ignored the twinge of pain and shrugged, 'I stopped trying when I turned twenty-one.'

Alessio shook his head, sliding away from yet another strong impulse to ease her pain. But he couldn't stop the words that came. 'In my experience, it's a decision he will regret before too long.'

The eyes that met his glittered in the festive lights but he still caught the despondency within the alluring grey. 'You have a crystal ball, do you?'

'No, but I turn down more requests to fix family reunions than I care to count. It's often misunderstood that I'm a fixer, not a priest or mediator.'

'Why do you turn them down? You don't like the emotional baggage that comes with it?'

His jaw clenched before he consciously eased it. 'Since the baggage belongs to them, not me, no, I don't. I turn them down because more often than not they, like your father, were in the wrong in the first place and want an easy passage to absolution.' His gaze drifted over her face, imprinting every feature deep in his mind.

'Well, I'm not holding my breath. And if he doesn't it's his loss.'

'Exactly so,' he concurred.

He held his coffee in one hand while his other spiked into her hair and cradled the back of her head. 'You've turned out to be an unexpected surprise in many ways, *duci.*'

She wasn't sure how to respond to that. Or to the bewilderment that preceded the flame lighting through his eyes. And, like so many terrifying things to do with this man and the seismic shifts he caused in her, she let herself be swept away by another kiss.

Then he was pulling away, determination stamped in his face as he nudged her back. 'Presents. Now. Then I have very definite ideas of how else you can wish me Merry Christmas.'

The first orb contained a platinum bracelet with a stunning sapphire stone in the middle. Then came a pair of diamond earrings. The third contained a QR code declaring it as a ticket to spend the day with—

Her jaw dropped when she read the renowned poet laureate's name.

'Alessio, I can't accept all this,' she protested after the twentieth priceless gem had fallen into her lap.

'You must. None of them are quite my type.'

Whose type are they? she wanted to ask. She didn't. Instead she raised an eyebrow. 'Not even the poet laureate?'

'I already met them after I ensured their favourite writing ink distributor didn't go out of business when the unfavourable economy threatened them.' At her gasp, his lips quirked in a shadowy smile, then he nudged a few more presents towards her. 'Be assured, *duci*, everything I need to make this a memorable *Natale* is well within my reach.'

She didn't need a crystal ball to know what he meant. But the knowledge twisted an ache in her heart and a graver comprehension that she was in much deeper than she wanted to be. That she already dreaded taking the road that led away from this place. Away from Alessio.

To hide the emotional earthquake juddering inside

her, she reached for the nearest globe. Then the next. Opening presents she had no intention of taking with her.

And then making a great show of throwing herself into a day she was certain would haunt her with its near perfection because of the man who resided in the centre of it.

A series of loud pings echoed across the room, making her startle out of her Boxing Day, front-of-the-fire-post-lovemaking haze.

She tried to turn but Alessio held her captive, his lips continuing their lazy exploration of her neck. 'Alessio.'

'Hmm. I think I'm addicted to the way you say my name. There's always a hint of exasperation in there that gives me great insight into how I affect you.'

'And that pleases you? Why am I surprised?'

His grin brushed her shoulder, and she tried desperately not to melt even though she suspected that, while her body might be willed into submission, her emotions were another matter entirely. She moaned as he licked at a particularly strong erogenous zone before his mouth drifted up to sear over hers. They were locked in another torrid kiss when another round of pings erupted into the air.

Alessio tensed slightly, the implications settling on both of them.

When he lifted his head, she sucked in a slow breath. 'The internet connection is back.' Why was there a hint of mourning in her words? Why did her heart sink a few feet too?

'Hmm.' This time, it wasn't the lazy purring of a

satisfied jungle animal. It was sharper, tinged with acceptance. Purpose, even.

When his lips left her skin, she fought not to beg him to return. To forget the outside world.

He had a vendetta to complete. And she…

She had a mother to appease. A sister to locate. A job to return to shortly after the new year.

For the first time in her life, though, not even the job she loved could pierce the gloom settling over her as Alessio rose to his feet in all his naked glory and crossed the room to where his phone had been discarded what felt like a lifetime ago.

His profile turned serious, then downright forbidding as he read the torrent of messages. She sat up, wrapping her arms around her knees as she watched him. She should get up too, go to her room and fetch her own phone and get on with the business of the rest of her life.

But she couldn't move. Didn't want to leave this enthralling little bubble created despite the acrimony pushing at it. Despite every rationale shrieking that it was the very worst of ideas.

Frozen, she watched Alessio's thumb hover over the screen. Then dark golden eyes rose to pierce hers. She wanted to believe indecision flitted across his face. A nanosecond later, when his digit pressed firmly, she knew she'd been mistaken.

The ring tone echoed loudly, the sound almost alien after so much time spent without its intrusion. Then a deep male voice was answering, and Alessio was lifting the device to his ear. *'Ciao.'*

The conversation was short, to the point.

Yes, he was fine. Yes, he required his helicopter as

quickly as it could be arranged to fetch them. And yes, they would be requiring his jet too to take them back to Sicily.

Them.

That finally roused Giada.

She surged to her feet as he finished the phone call. He stared at her with his hands on his lean hips.

'My Sicilian isn't great, but did I hear you tell them that you're returning to Sicily with me?'

He strolled in that loose-limbed way that made her insides turn liquid. When he reached her, he cupped her shoulders, before his fingers drifted up to spear into her hair. '*Se*, you did. Wasn't that what we agreed?'

She frowned. 'But I thought…' She'd agreed to this when he didn't know her true identity.

He lifted an eyebrow. 'You thought what?' Hardness had crept into his tone, the fingers in her hair applying slight pressure, a subtle warning.

A tremor awoke deep in her belly, the stirring of old anguish wearing a new face. 'You know now that I'm not Gigi. Surely you won't achieve anything by keeping me with you?'

Hardness settled in deep, sculpting his face into a chilling work of art without him moving a single muscle. For an age, he stared at her, strands of disappointment and almost pity weaving through those golden eyes before he slid his thumb slowly, contemplatively over her bottom lip. 'You think, because we've had the pleasure of each other's bodies, that anything has changed, *bedda mia*? That I should simply abandon my life's goal?'

Anguish intensified, mocking her for having the temerity to believe it would ever die. For daring to think that she had the power to move a man like him to alter his path. But, even if she didn't—and she realised now that it'd been a foolish dream—she still wouldn't hold her tongue.

'Do you hear yourself? How can this be your life's goal? You have so much already, the very world at your feet. Why can't you strive for reconciliation? For peace? For forgiveness? For...love?'

He stiffened into pure steel, his nostrils flaring before he surged closer still, their breaths mingling as he looked deep into her eyes. 'How can I find peace when those responsible for shattering my family still walk free?'

Her insides clenched, partly with sympathy, but mostly for the raw, unvarnished pain that bricked his voice. 'Alessio—'

His hands dropped from her as if he couldn't bear her touch any longer. 'I made a promise, Giada! And I mean to keep it.'

It wasn't a roar of intent, but the boom of it blasted through her nevertheless. And as she took one breath after the next, battling against the horrible, terrifying notion that she wasn't merely attempting to be the rock he needed but to form the foundation of what she yearned for with him, Giada realised there was nothing she could say. Nothing she could do.

She'd strayed so far from her usual tormented path, wandered much farther than she should've, that she barely recognised this new, more desolate landscape.

'I understand,' she said, not understanding entirely. Perhaps because even though he'd helped her reconcile herself to the possibility that hers was meant to be a fractured family, she couldn't do the same for him. Couldn't help him see beyond the red haze of the pain and grieving for everything he'd lost. 'But you should really ask yourself this—did the father who loved you and taught you a life of integrity and honour want you to lower yourself to the level of the very people who betrayed him, or would he want you to choose a different path? And would your mother have extracted that vow from you if she hadn't been blind with grief?'

His fists bunched and the brackets around his mouth tightened as he stared down at her, icily condemning her.

She raised her hand before he could flay her with words. 'I know you think I have no right, but isn't there a saying about an eye for an eye making the whole world blind?'

'Are you really preaching at me about turning the other cheek?'

She shrugged. 'Why not? I don't have anything to lose, do I?'

'You think not?'

She forced a smile she didn't feel. 'I have a few more days to spare. I'll come with you to Sicily. Let you toss me into another room so you can feel good about staying true to your vows and whatnot. Once Gigi returns your precious crest, we'll be truly done with each other. Does that work for you?'

He looked momentarily nonplussed, as if she'd disrupted his grand and mighty chessboard game and ruined his plans. If her insides hadn't been ripping apart slowly at the stark realisation that she would indeed be walking away from this man in a matter of days with a heart she suspected didn't belong to her in its entirety, she would've laughed.

Would've indulged one last time in the touching and banter and ease they'd found in the last few days. In the best Christmas she'd ever had.

Denied that—and knowing more heartache awaited, because hadn't she ignored all the warnings, breezily believed she could master these emotions?—she turned and walked out of the living room.

She didn't expect him to stop her and of course he didn't.

Their unplanned interlude was over.

He had an illustrious quest to complete, and she…

Giada swallowed hard, her steps quickening on the stairs, not because she was in a tearing hurry, but because she feared she'd be unable to suppress the sobs frothing up her chest, eager to vocalise her shattered emotions.

She made it to her room as the first one choked out of her. She clenched her jaw shut, furious with herself for this inability to rise above torment that shouldn't have been there in the first place.

Crossing the room, she dug out her phone and turned it on.

The void while she waited for it to power up felt like an eternity. But when it was done and only three meagre pings sounded, Giada wished she'd waited until she had herself under better control. Until she'd applied sound reasoning to everything that had happened to her and bolstered herself with every *I will survive* speech she could think up.

Then she would've been better prepared to accept there was no hope for the shattered family she'd been cursed with. Because only two further text messages awaited her.

After nearly two weeks since leaving London and having minimal contact with her sister. The first message she'd already seen when the internet briefly returned. The second came on Christmas Eve.

Renata says you're not joining her for Xmas? Are you still with him? WTH? Call me. G

Giada reread the second message, incredulity building when it registered that her sister was more irritated that she hadn't made it home for Christmas and was still with Alessio. There was a searing disbelief that Gigi could be this self-centred. That maybe Alessio was right. She'd made far too many excuses for her sister in the past. Sucking in a breath, she clicked on the third message. Sent on Christmas Day.

Call me now, Gids. Not sure what you're playing at! G

A sharp bark of incredulous laughter left her throat. She stopped the next one for fear it would turn into something else, like hysterical screaming.

Jaw gritted, she hit the call button. And listened to it ring and ring, then click into voicemail. Giada cleared her throat. 'Hey, it's me.' She paused, her mind replaying everything that had happened since she last spoke to her sister, shaking her head when her emotions started to swell out of control again.

'I…we got stuck in a snowstorm…in Alessio's chalet.' She gave a quick, impersonal summary, leaving out the bits about her sleeping with the man she'd been sent to deceive. 'Anyway, call me when you get this message. And please tell me you've located his crest.' She paused, swallowed and delivered the last, most important news. 'And, Gigi, Alessio knows I'm not you. I don't know what that means for you, but please return his item. It's more important to him than you know.'

She ended the call, her heart thudding dully in her chest. Then, feeling his presence behind her, Giada turned to find a fully dressed Alessio in the doorway, his eyes burning into her.

She didn't need to ask him if he'd heard any of what she'd said. It blazed right there in his eyes as he watched her toss the phone on the bed.

'I take it you didn't reach your sister?'

'You don't need to lurk in doorways listening to my calls, Alessio. That's beneath you.'

Her probably unfair dig bounced off his shoulders, his hands slotting into his pockets as he leaned his magnificent frame in the doorway. 'But then how would I gain all the delicious information that serves me so well, *bedda mia*?'

The endearment threatened to weaken her knees, the way it had every time he'd drawled it. But the mockery attached to it steeled her spine. Kept her on track. 'No, I didn't reach her, but I'm sure she'll call back as soon as she hears my message.'

Heavy scepticism crossed his face. 'What will it take to lose this blind faith you have in her?'

She scrubbed her fingers through her hair, her emotions rushing wildly beneath her skin. 'Feel free to take the high road on what you think is right for your family, but don't you dare look down your nose at me for whatever you think are my shortcomings. Your opinions aren't wanted or appreciated. Now, is there something you want particularly, or can I assume this conversation over?'

He stiffened, then he straightened, his body filling the doorway. Slowly, he sauntered into the room. Her breath caught as he came closer, his gaze ablaze with the kind of righteous purpose superior beings possessed.

'There is such a thing as being far too accommodating, you know, *cara*?' he warned silkily.

She met his gaze boldly, because she sensed if she didn't, she would simply succumb to the tsunami of emotions churning ever closer. 'Are you annoyed about that because it's not directed at you? That I have the capacity to care about more than one person?'

His nostrils flared and she realised she'd scored a bullseye. Whatever this man denied he wanted from her, he wasn't quite ready to see her give it away to someone else. That thought brought a shocked laugh. 'You are, aren't you? Why is that?'

'Because I've seen first-hand what happens when people think you're a soft touch. They will take and take and take until there's nothing left.'

'So your answer is to stop yourself from giving anything at all?' Her question was softly spoken, something inside *still* vulnerable for him. Enough to tread lightly with his wild emotions. 'To hold everything inside until it shrivels to nothing and dies? Is that really how you want to live, Alessio?'

'This isn't about—'

'You? Of course it is. You're hiding. And you're condemning everyone who isn't hiding like you.'

Just like in the living room, his expression flashed with bewilderment. Then he shook his head, freed himself from the feeling gripping him. Even before he spoke, she knew he was going to distance himself once more.

'Contrary to what you think, I didn't come to eavesdrop on your call but to inform you there's a window for our departure. My helicopter will be here in two hours. Make sure you're ready to leave.'

CHAPTER TEN

YOU'RE HIDING.

Alessio seethed at the words spinning in his head in sync with the helicopter's rotor blades above him. He didn't even bother wondering how she dared lay such accusations on him when no one else would be brave enough to speak to him that way. Dr Giada Parker had a streak of fearlessness and an unwavering spirit that had drawn him right from the start.

But she was talking nonsense, of course. Especially when her own record was so woeful.

The more in-depth report he'd finally been able to access about Gigi Parker—and the fact that she had a twin sister along with their Italian mother—when the internet was restored painted a vivid picture of the Parker family. They weren't as brutal as his own family, but the lifestyles of two out of the three made for unsavoury reading.

And yet... Giada had never once turned her back on her sister and mother, and even made excuses for their dysfunction.

As unworthy as they were, she'd do anything for them.

A puzzling, guilt-tinged sensation made him shift

in his seat. When the compulsion grew too much, he slanted a glance at her.

Her hands were tucked neatly in her lap, her steady gaze on the endlessly white landscape. While it grated how easily she could ignore and dismiss him, he took advantage of it to break down just what it was about her that riled him so, starting with the differences with her twin. *Dio mio*, if everything he'd read was right, she was as different from her sister and mother as night was from day.

Her sister was living proof of the apple not falling far from the tree.

As for Renata DiMarco...

Alessio's growing fury at the distress caused by her mother was another surprising discovery, and it'd recurred enough for him to weather the bewilderment a little better. To accept that maybe this was par for the course when dealing with Giada.

Once they parted ways...

The thought screeched to a halt in his brain, his belly clenching in rejection of it.

Yes, he reeled a little at how differently Giada had turned out in comparison to the rest of her family. But it didn't grant her the right to issue judgements about him. He didn't care, he assured himself. Not when all his meticulous machinations were bearing fruit, even while he'd been snowbound with his duplicitous guest.

His uncles were *finally* feeling the pinch of the traps Alessio had set for them, some of them years in the making—they'd proved a slippery, elusive lot with more cunning than he'd anticipated—with more than half of their shady endeavours hitting the rocks. With the remaining soon to follow, the first tentative attempts at contact had already begun. It was even more imperative now that the Cresta Montaldi be returned.

The fire of anticipation burned bright, yet hollow at the thought that the years of plotting and planning were nearing an end. He could, *finally*, look forward to a new year with a clean slate. A new year with his family name restored and those culpable paying the appropriate price for their sins.

Hell, he might even consider an extended liaison with her…

No.

He removed his gaze from her smooth cheek and sleek neck when it registered he'd been staring at her long enough to draw a querying eyebrow at him. Long enough for that telltale blush that should've been a dead giveaway when they met to climb into her face. He balled his fist on his thigh when the urge to touch her unleashed another bout of hunger.

No. This was over.

Does it need to be?

He sucked in a breath when his gaze drifted to her again, to her pink lips, slightly parted as she took shallow breaths.

'Is there a reason you keep staring at me?' she enquired, but he caught traces of breathlessness, the touch of bewilderment he himself felt. As if what was happening between them was as peculiar to her as it was to him.

He was an expert fixer, arguably the best in the world, and yet he couldn't solve the conundrum of Dr Giada Parker and the riotous feelings she roused inside him.

Shelving the subject for now, he glanced out of the window, relieved to see the airport come into view. The sooner he got back to Palermo, the sooner everything would slot back into its rightful place.

'You look cold,' he said, evading her question. He couldn't very well admit that she captivated him on a level no other woman had been able to achieve. That even now, he couldn't go a minute without wanting to look at her…to touch her.

But she was an addiction he *would* break.

He shrugged out of his coat, ignoring her budding frown when he draped it over her shoulders. 'We're landing in five minutes. And in case you haven't noticed, the temperatures are still negative digits out there.' Alessio couldn't stop the mild punch of primitive satisfaction when her fingers gripped the lapels and drew them closer to her body. 'And next time you decide on another identity-switching escapade, perhaps you should put your foot down about packing more sensible clothes?'

'You have enough on your plate, Signor Montaldi. Let me worry about how I dress in future.' The saccharine smile she tagged on made him want to kiss her mouth all the more desperately, then drag a promise from her that she would never put herself in a similar situation for her undeserving sister again.

But he suspected his tigress would bite his head off. She was fierce when it came to her family.

Just…as *he* was.

He sucked another breath as that singular truth dug deeper into him. And for the rest of their transfer from chopper to plane and through the myriad phone calls he had to field while they flew to their destination, Alessio couldn't dispel the notion that they weren't so dissimilar after all.

* * *

Giada pressed her phone to her ear for the sixth time since she boarded Alessio's luxury private jet. She'd wanted to be relieved that he'd barely waited until take-off before disappearing through a door at the rear of the plane. But all she'd felt was increasing anxiety and a harrowing *loss* as they flew towards Sicily.

She'd seen the looks the airport staff and Alessio's employees had cast her in the VIP lounge and as she'd boarded his airplane. Now she was no longer playing a part and consumed with getting her sister out of trouble, she was even more aware of how out of his league she was. No amount of reassuring herself that she didn't care worked any more.

And he was taking her to the heart of his existence.

As much as she knew he put up a formidable façade, Giada had seen enough cracks to glimpse the pain that resided beneath that front. Having accepted that she *did* care, she feared her heart had different ideas. The foolish organ wanted to shield him, maybe even herself, from the true torment his vendetta had and would cost Alessio Montaldi.

So she kept calling Gigi. Kept leaving messages.

She was in the middle of leaving yet another when she felt him approach. Her very skin tingled and shivered, and her heart leapt in such an alarming way, Giada was already dreading looking at him.

Just as she was dreading looking deeper into the depth of her heart's desire when it came to Alessio. A desire she suspected had scaled the ultimate emotion…

But that same compulsive yearning made her lift her gaze to the man with his hands in his pockets, regarding her from a seat away. Whose gaze searched hers with an intensity she wanted to scream at.

When that gaze dropped down to the phone clutched in her hand, she was almost relieved. Until he spoke.

'If you're trying to reach your sister, don't bother. She's not going to answer.'

Anxiety tore through her. 'Why not? What have you done?' she snapped.

His features hardened. A muscle ticced in his jaw. 'I see you continue to think the worst of me. Does it give you satisfaction to do so?'

The silky query was at odds with the censure gleaming in his eyes. Giada felt a momentary pang of regret.

'I'm sorry, I shouldn't have automatically assumed. But I still want an answer. What's…where's Gigi? How do you know she's not going to answer?' Fear crawled up her throat as the questions spilled out.

Alessio advanced and sat down opposite her. 'She's unharmed.' His face twisted with that disdain she hadn't seen since before Christmas. Seeing it again sent a pulse of dismay through her. It didn't matter, she told herself. All she cared about was Gigi. But she knew it was a lie as the hollow widened in her belly. 'She's been seen with a particularly unsavoury group in the South of France, hired by two of my uncles. The initial report is that she isn't there willingly.'

Giada jerked forward in her seat. 'What? Why?'

Another twist of contemptuous fury. 'It looks like she trusted the wrong people.' He shrugged. 'Or she's clueless as to who they truly are. Who knows?'

'And? What aren't you telling me?'

For an age, he simply stared at her. '*They*, and not

your sister, are in possession of my crest. I suspect she's not answering your calls because she's unwilling to be forthcoming about the true prospects of recovering what she took.'

'But she can't…she wouldn't just…' She shook her head. 'You said unsavoury. Just how unsavoury and why don't you look more worried about your chances of getting back your property?'

The look that entered his eyes left her without a doubt as to the true nature of the man she was dealing with. 'The information is still coming in about your sister. As for worrying about my chances…' He gave an expressive shrug. 'You forget that I'm a fixer, Giada. Which means I always come out on top, especially where my own interests are concerned. My property *will* be recovered.'

She didn't doubt him for a moment. So far only the most extreme kind of *force majeure* had stood in his way. 'And what about Gigi?' She hated how her voice trembled. Hated how she feared his answer because it would break her heart.

His eyes turned into hard chips. 'I suspect she'll resurface when she believes the coast is clear. But our deal still holds, *duci*. You won't leave my sight until the Cresta Montaldi is in my hands, *se*?'

Giada was certain she should've been more outraged than she actually felt. But a numbness was overcoming her. And it had nothing to do with discovering what her sister had been up to. Or even Alessio's insistence on keeping her captive. No, it was more to do with how she felt about Alessio Montaldi. And the absolute certainty that he would shatter her before this was over. But her breaking heart still held enough concern and love for her twin. Enough for her to ask, 'Is Gigi safe?'

'At the last report she was fine,' he said coolly as an attendant approached to inform them they would be landing soon.

The drive from the airport to the Montaldi estate near Monreale was swift and conducted in silence on her part, and with rapier-sharp Sicilian conversation on Alessio's. At some point he switched to French, then to German. From the snippets she could grasp, several irons he'd placed in his fire before being snowbound with her were ready.

But despite the flash of triumph on his face after each call ended, he grew tenser as they passed beneath what looked like a caretaker's residence spread over towering iron gates.

Giada grasped the reason for the grand entrance when, after three heart-racing minutes driving along a tree-lined stone drive, an honest to goodness eighteenth-century castle unfolded into view.

Complete with battlements, turrets and pointed arches, it was straight out of a neo-Gothic fairy tale.

'Welcome to Castello Montaldi.' The throb of pride in his voice didn't defuse his tension as he threw open his door and held out his hand to her.

Giada followed him up a porticoed entrance and into a jaw-dropping marble foyer, determined not to be overwhelmed.

A single step later, she knew it was a lost cause. Everywhere she looked, Alessio's proud heritage loomed.

'I need to attend to a few things. Vincenza will show

you to your room.' A middle-aged woman with a kind smile and greying hair stepped forward, her clothing and bearing marking her as the housekeeper. Alessio started to turn away, then veered back. 'Vincenza will also help you pick an attire for tonight. I've had a few delivered for you.'

'What's happening tonight?' she asked.

A hard little smile lifted his lips. 'A family party. You'll be attending as my guest, of course.'

Giada wanted to shout at him to come back. To curse him for springing this unwanted surprise on her. But she feared it would fall on deaf ears. Or worse, that she'd dissolve into hysterics. How foolish had she been to think leaving their snowbound chalet behind would mean the end of this roller coaster?

And how especially foolish was she to experience that lingering thrill that she would spend at least another day with Alessio before—?

The bracing reminder of Gigi's plight shaved off several layers of her traitorous feelings as she followed Vincenza up one set of sweeping stairs.

'The *castello* is big, *signora*, so it will be better if a maid stays close by to bring you where you need to go, *se*?' Vincenza smiled when Giada nodded.

Several hallways later and a brief history that informed her there were nineteen bedrooms, a chapel, and a private park on the estate among many other eye-goggling facts, double doors opened into a stunning stone-walled room, complete with four-poster, antique sofas she was sure were as old as the *castello*, and blood-red velvet drapes tied back with gold rope.

And at the foot of her bed, a rail of exquisite gowns

waited on hangers. A glimpse of the labels made her eyes widen, although, in hindsight, she shouldn't have been surprised.

She nodded through the quick tour of her suite, then as Vincenza prepared to leave after promising a tray of refreshments, Giada cleared her throat. 'Is the party for a specific reason or is it a yearly thing?'

Vincenza hesitated, then her eyes shadowed a little. 'The Montaldi Christmas ball is a tradition started by his *matri* that Signor Alessio continues.'

A *ball*, not a party. Damn Alessio. 'I see.' Her gaze drifted back to the gowns. 'And what time am I to be ready?' she asked.

'It starts at seven. I'll return to help you get dressed,' Vincenza replied.

She wanted to tell the older woman not to bother, that she could dress herself, but something held her tongue. Alessio's tension suggested this wasn't just another traditional holiday event. The last thing Giada wanted was to compound her sins.

She murmured her thanks, and when the tray arrived, she nibbled on olives, parcelled meats and pastries, washed down with a gorgeous chilled limoncello. Then she took a long, leisurely bath, attempting not to succumb to the growing anxiety at Gigi's continued radio silence.

She chose the blood-orange velvet gown because it was festive, she told herself. Not because the Montaldi coat of arms she'd seen stamped on various items throughout her suite bore the same colour.

Vincenza's smile of approval when she saw Giada's choice eased her growing jitters. And by the time the older woman had expertly coiled and woven Giada's newly shampooed ash-blonde hair into an elaborate chignon, it was impossible not to feel a resurgence of overwhelming sensation.

Dragging her gaze from the woman in the full-length gilt-edged mirror, who was at once familiar and alien to her, Giada smiled at Vincenza. 'Thank you for your help.'

The housekeeper returned her smile, then reached for the velvet pouch she'd brought with her. 'From Signor Alessio. For you to wear, then meet him downstairs.'

Giada spun to face her. 'What is it?'

Vincenza pulled out a squat jewellery box and deftly flipped it open. Giada gasped. If she'd thought the perfect little gems from the chalet were breathtaking, this was on another level. The ruby and diamond necklace winked and sparkled its brilliance from its velvet bed. And, damn it all, it was perfect for the dress she'd chosen.

Giada thought of refusing but as quickly as the denial rose, she squashed it. There was no point.

Just as she'd left those treasures behind, she would merely use this for whatever part she needed to play until Gigi resurfaced. So she bit her lip and nodded at Vincenza, who smiled enthusiastically and fastened the necklace and matching earrings in place.

Checking her phone one last time and gritting her teeth at her sister's silence, she followed the housekeeper.

It was testament to the size of the *castello* that Giada hadn't seen or heard any signs of the ball beginning until they descended onto the ground floor and traversed a series of hallways.

Then she heard the strains of classical music.

'*Buonasera, duci,*' his deep voice murmured just behind her shoulder.

Giada spun around, her breath catching as she blinked at Alessio while his gaze raked her from head to toe.

'You look sensational,' he rasped heavily.

He looked sublime. Naturally. The soot-black tuxedo emphasised his physical perfection, the styled-back hair lending him an air of sexy danger that had her insides knotting with dizzy desire, her heart searching for a way out of a prison that had lost its key somewhere on the snow-covered peaks of Gris-Montana.

Because as her gaze collided with his, as she witnessed the heat and the anguish and the danger and realised that, alongside it, the shadows had grown, that tension from earlier had only intensified in the hours they'd been apart, Giada understood that she would do anything to take his torment away.

Because she loved him.

And when that crucial truth strangled her vocal cords, leaving her mute as he stepped closer, placed a finger beneath her chin to lift her face to his, she surrendered to the feeling. Because to fight it here and now was to bare it all to him.

To show him what her foolish heart had done.

'It's time.'

She forced herself to focus. 'Time for what?' she asked distractedly.

Darkness shrouded his face, and his jaw turned to stone as he offered her his elbow. 'Time to put beloved ghosts to rest, finally.'

He *needed* to do this.

Otherwise, what would've been the point of his life

up till now? What would the years of scheming and sacrifice have been for?

Maybe it's time to let it go...

Similar words to the ones *she'd* spoken...*traitorous* words...this time spoken by his own brother a mere hour ago. Tonight of all nights, when he'd finally confirmed that every shady enterprise and support his uncles had relied on was dismantled and they were well and truly broken, when vengeance was within his grasp? When one uncle had fled Sicily and two others were here tonight, their tails between their legs, eager for his forgiveness?

Entering the ballroom now and seeing Massimo's half-pleading look made Alessio's gut tighten.

If he hadn't taken them at their word that they'd never met before, he would've believed the stunning Dr Parker and his brother were ganging up on him, breaking down defences he suddenly lacked the willpower to uphold.

Because what was worst of all? He'd entertained the possibility of *letting go* for a full minute, and, *santo cielo*, the lightness of being had taken his breath away.

But in that brief abandonment of his life's purpose, other *unattainable* yearnings had rushed in, tormenting him with impossible mirages of what his life could look like.

With Giada Parker.

With...love?

That was when he knew it would never happen. Because the ferocity of his need in that minute? It surpassed every crumb of vengeance he'd gathered to himself over the years. And it...terrified him.

So no, there would be no *letting it go*. Not even knowing deep in his bones that his mother was already resting easier knowing his crest was back in his possession, their family honour and respect well within reach.

Letting go meant being unmoored. Being alone.

And for the first time in his life, Alessio wasn't quite ready to face a challenge.

Cold dread seized Giada's nape as the ballroom doors swung open and several dozen heads swivelled their way.

Her fingers dug reflexively into Alessio's arm. He made a low noise in his throat but he didn't slow his steps. On the contrary, he all but dragged her after him, his fierce gaze cutting through his own guests as if they weren't there.

Someone approached with champagne. Giada took the glass just for something to occupy her. And when her eyes sought Alessio again, his tension had escalated even more.

'Alessio—'

'There you are, *frati*. I was beginning to think you wouldn't show.'

Giada turned towards the only person who'd dared to venture close, her eyes widening as she registered the man's resemblance to Alessio.

'Massimo,' Alessio bit out, confirming who the younger man was.

Massimo nodded at his brother, then his gaze shifted to her. 'I understand I'm to blame for you getting stuck with my brother.' Eyes a shade lighter than his brother's glinted beneath the ballroom chandeliers. 'Do I need to beg your forgiveness or—?'

'Is everything in place?' Alessio snapped, his jaw hard enough to crunch titanium.

Massimo's gaze flicked away from hers, a hint of hardness and something else…something she wanted to label compassion shifting through the gold depths as he looked at his brother. '*Se, frati.* Are you sure you want to do this? We can—'

'I'm sure,' Alessio interrupted.

Massimo paused a beat, then nodded at someone behind Alessio's shoulder. A man holding a large box under his arm stepped up to the dais where a quartet played.

When the music trailed off, Alessio eased her arm from his. Without glancing her way, he stepped up to the dais. A second later, Massimo trailed him and stood one step below.

Giada's heart thumped hard as a hush came over the crowd, their gazes commanded by their host.

'Everyone here is connected in some way to my family. So you'll know some or all of our history. You'll know the wrong that has been done to us.' He paused, his eyes narrowing as they tracked across the room. 'Some of those traitors are here tonight.' At the gasps that sounded, he smiled. 'They eat and drink from my table and dare to hope that I've forgotten. I…' his gaze darted to Massimo '…*we* haven't forgotten.' He gestured with his hand and the man with the box stepped forward.

Even before he'd opened it, Giada knew what it contained.

Sure enough, when Alessio lifted the lid to the sizeable antique box, the most exquisite ruby-and-emerald-encrusted crest about the size of a large dinner plate, the same winged roaring lions design as the monogrammed items she'd seen all over the *castello*, nestled on the blood-orange silk bed. He plucked it out and held it up almost indifferently, but the slight tremble of his hand and the ferocious look in his eyes relayed his tumult.

'Tonight, with this *cresta* returned to us, my brother and I reclaim our birthright, and I my place as the rightful head of the Montaldi family. Anyone who disagrees, speak now.'

A rumble tore through the room, but no one dared raise a voice.

Alessio gave a satisfied nod, then continued, 'We also claim the right to seek justice the way we see fit. The culprits know who they are. Present yourselves.'

The crowd slowly parted to reveal two grey-haired older men. They were a poor likeness of what Alessio would look like thirty years from now but the resemblance was patent. Giada had no doubt they were his uncles.

They lurched towards Alessio, hushed pleas falling from their lips. When they got close enough, they grasped Alessio's hand, dropped frantic kisses on it.

Alessio's livid gaze fixed on them, then unerringly found Giada's.

Perhaps she mouthed the *no*. Perhaps she only screamed it in her head. Either way, Alessio's eyes darkened, determination warring with bewilderment. His chest heaved frantically for a full minute. Then he stepped off the dais, leaving his uncles kneeling on the floor.

And he left the ballroom.

Giada knew if she didn't go after him, she'd lose him in the labyrinthian *castello*. At least that was the surface truth she told herself. The deeper one was the unrelenting need to take away his pain. To offer solace. So when she saw his tall figure stride down one hallway and enter what looked like a study, she tore after him. Only to pause in the doorway when she realised he was on the phone.

'And the Parker woman?' he rasped.

Giada's heart lurched, then grasped that he wasn't necessarily talking about her. He confirmed it a moment later. 'The deal was for the return of my property. Nothing else. She found her way into this mess. She can find her way out of it.'

Giada stumbled forward, unable to remain quiet. 'What are you talking about? Is it something to do with Gigi?'

Alessio swung around. The look in his eyes hadn't dissipated one iota. In that moment he was a man locked in full vendetta mode.

'Answer me, Alessio!'

He continued to regard her like a speck of dust on his clothing.

Then he reached for the door and shut it in her face.

When her shock wore off, Giada reached for the handle, then banged on the door when it didn't budge. 'Alessio!'

His voice rumbled on for another minute before he yanked the door open. He was no longer on the phone.

'What do you want, Dr Parker?' His voice was soft, tinged with fury.

Giada rushed into the room. 'What's going on? Who were you talking to? Call them back!'

'I will not. Your sister is no longer of interest to me. She's been warned never to cross my path again.'

A shaky breath exploded from her. 'You really are a cold bastard, aren't you?'

'Not at all. I think I've been exceedingly magnanimous in not having her thrown in jail.' He strolled to the window, then retraced his steps back to her. 'And I'm prepared to extend that generosity to you.'

For one foolish, traitorous moment her heart leapt. Then the true meaning of his words imploded within her. 'To me?' she repeated.

'*Se.* You. I have zero interest in anyone else.'

She was grappling with the singularly vicious delivery when he continued, 'Since we've established that we're not entirely averse to each other's company, I'd like you to stay here in Palermo with me until the new year.'

The dark temptation in his voice, coupled with the trailing of his fingers over her jaw and down her neck to her shoulder, *almost* made her succumb.

'You really don't get it, do you? I can never be with a man who throws people away the way you do. So the answer is no. I won't be rolling around in bed with you while my sister's safety hangs in the balance. Whether it's her fault or not, I'm going after her. And I expect you to honour your offer not to call the cops on me. Or was that an empty promise? Because I'm leaving this place. As soon as you tell me where to find my sister.'

Giada could've sworn he'd paled a little; that he sucked in the smallest shocked breath, as if her outburst had thrown him. But when she searched for a chink in his formidable façade all that was reflected back at her was chilling indifference. Which he shored up with a shrug.

'If that's the way you feel—'

'It is,' she tossed back quickly. Because that flood of emotion was building again, threatening to weaken her the longer she stayed in his presence. And she was done being weak for this man. Done trying to make him see that the fervour with which he cherished his family was the same for her.

Could be the same fervour for each other.

'An address will be provided for you by the time your belongings are packed,' he said icily, then retreated to the window, his broad back a stone wall.

Giada's head spun with how swiftly everything was falling apart. She could barely remember the walk from study to bedroom. Could barely recollect shoving her clothes into her suitcase. But as she left the dressing room, she caught sight of herself in the mirror. She still wore her gown.

And the ruby and diamond necklace and earrings.

A half-sob threatened to escape. She swallowed it down forcefully, dropping her case so she could tackle the clasp.

It refused to budge a full ten minutes later. Giada stifled a tiny scream, the fever rushing through her bearing all the hallmarks of hysteria.

Dear God, if this was what love did to rational beings, she didn't want it.

Liar. You want it with every fibre of your being. And you want it with the man who's just broken your heart!

Another sob caught in her throat. She exhaled it in relief when she heard footsteps behind her. 'Vincenza, thank God. Can you get this necklace off me, please?'

Warm hands clasped her shoulders, making her yelp as Alessio breathed in her ear. 'Not yet. I've decided we're not quite done. I have some further things to say.'

'Are you serious? We have nothing to say to one another. Not after—'

The words died in her throat when she spun around and saw the anguish etched on his face.

'All this is your fault. You know that, don't you?' he accused thickly.

'Oh, yes, I'm aware that blame has landed on my lap since we met. But maybe you'd care to elaborate?'

His nostrils flared. 'In a matter of days, you've made me need so badly. I trained myself not to do that after my father died. Then I redoubled my efforts when I lost my mother. But you, *duci*. You...' He gave her shoulders a gentle shake. 'Don't you understand what you've done? Tonight I abandoned every vow I made, in the name of *mercy*. I told you I wanted nothing to do with your sister and yet I've just negotiated her release and put myself in debt to some objectionable individuals. She's on her way home and has promised to call you twice a week from now on until you say otherwise.'

He laughed harshly as she gasped, grateful tears springing to her eyes as he released her to drag shaking fingers through his hair. 'Nobody else gets a chance like this with me. No one else would get this far. If word of this gets out, my reputation will be in shreds,' he accused.

And yet there was no venom in his tone. If anything, Alessio Montaldi looked shell-shocked and a little vulnerable at the revelation.

The light that shone in his eyes was almost...pleading.

'What am I going to do now?' It was a hushed query, his eyes searching hers for answers. 'I've dismantled every nefarious dealing my uncles profited from. I have them in the palm of my hand. But I can't bring myself to crush them. And, *Diu mio*, I find myself considering granting them forgiveness. You've ruined me, Dr Parker.'

Her heart gave a wild leap. 'Have I? Or have you proved to yourself that you are and were the better man all along? That you're truly your father's son? Now you get to truly live. You get to remember your parents for the wonderful people they were without the burden of vengeance weighing you down. You get to love free and true…if that's what you want.'

'And what about who I want? What if it's too late for me…with her?'

Agitation rolled through her belly, decades-old fear attempting to take hold once more. But he'd taught her to be brave. So she would be brave, *for them*. She'd stare the possibility of rejection in the face, one more time, and take the greatest risk of her life. 'You're a fixer, the great and fearsome Alessio Montaldi. Are you going to let the possibility stop you?'

His hand dropped slowly from where he'd clutched his nape. Eyes like gold lava stared into hers and his shoulders squared. He looked larger than life, but then, didn't he always? And yet, this time his mouth worked as if he was summoning up and testing words he was afraid to say.

Her heart lurched, fearful but eager. Willing him to say them. Because if he didn't…

She shook her head. *I trust you.*

She didn't realise she'd spoken the three little words out loud until his breath shuddered out of him.

'*Diu mio*, I don't deserve you. Or your trust.'

Her heart dropped six feet beneath her feet but she wasn't going to crumble. 'Why not?'

For the first time since she'd known him, shame and regret etched his face, sinking in deep as he shook his head. 'Because I *hesitated*, Giada. You asked me to save someone you love, and I hesitated because I was afraid. For myself. I was afraid what letting go would mean for me.'

She shook her head, puzzled. 'W-what do you mean?'

'Because it became clear that I would do *anything* for you. That I would lay down my very life for you if it came to it. I'm used to power and a lot of it. But…that sort of power, the kind you have over me, it's…'

'Terrifying?' she offered softly.

He made a rough, wholly animalistic sound at the back of his throat. *'Se,'* he agreed with an awed rasp.

'I guess that's that, then?' she dared. Then turned away.

He arrived in front of her with the force of a hurricane. Flames leapt in his eyes as he grabbed and held onto her upper arms. 'What?'

She shrugged even as her heart attempted to beat right out of her chest. 'If you're too terrified to face that power, then there's nothing more to discuss, is there?' She deliberately glanced at the door behind him. 'Maybe I'll take a holiday until my next posting. Find a man who—'

His untamed growl silenced her. 'I've just put one *vinnitta* behind me, *tesoro*. Do not let me pick up another.'

'There he is, my powerful Alessio. Are you going to do what it takes, then?' she teased.

His arms dragged her closer. 'Is this what you want? To see me at my most terrified? My most vulnerable?

To know that I love you so much, that I'm besotted to a level that petrifies me?' The words were jagged, almost broken. And the tremble that seized him when he said them made her heart surge with emotion.

Giada lifted her hands, slowly because the wildness in his eyes needed to be handled with care. He was a man on the brink.

The brink of a discovery so deep it terrified her too.

'Yes, I do,' she stated without holding back. And when she saw the jaw-dropping shock in his eyes, she smiled and cradled his strong jaw, rubbing her thumbs over his stubbled skin, revelling in the shudder that went through him. 'Before you go thinking me cruel, just know that I want you this way, this open and honest and fearful, because it means you'll treasure the feeling. Just as you treasured the memory of your parents, you'll fight every day to keep this feeling alive because you'll know that it's returned. With an equally open and honest heart, Alessio.'

The shuddering grew until a relentless wave overtook him, his eyes darkening until they were barely gold, until they burnished with disbelief and then hope. Joy. Awe. 'Giada…'

'I lo—'

'No.' His fingers brushed over her lips. 'Before you say words I might be too selfish to allow you to take back, you need to be sure, *duci*. Once I grab hold of a thing, I tend not to let it go. I might get obsessive. I might rage and burn a few worlds down for it. You saw how I was with my vow to my mother. I hesitated and almost sacrificed someone you love.'

The last words were dredged from a harrowing place she knew anguished him now.

'Do you regret it?' she asked.

His face twisted. 'Every second since, *tesoro*. I'll regret for the rest of my miserable life.'

'Doesn't that tell you anything, Alessio? Because it tells me that you know where you went wrong. That it was a single-second mistake instead of a decision you acted on even though you knew it would hurt me. And don't forget, you still got her back. Life is a complicated puzzle we work through every day. You can't close yourself to love because of a mistake you made. And even if you do, I'll still forgive you for it.'

He swallowed, his chest heaving in a deep breath. 'I still think—'

'Mention that you're not worthy of me one more time and I'll walk out of here.'

His eyes flared again. Then started to lighten, the flames leaping higher. 'I love you, Giada. With every undeserving bone in my body, I swear I will earn your love. I will never make you feel unsure of my devotion. Bless me with your heart and I will make you a vow to treasure it as long as I live.' The smallest hint of a wicked smile twitched his lips. 'And I think by now you know how I am with vows.'

Tears filled her eyes again and she *finally* let hope soar. 'I do. And yes. To all of it. We will love each other and embrace the fear. And when our children are born, we will show them that love like that is worth it, a hundred times over.'

His throat moved again and he shook his head. 'I didn't believe in fate or luck. But I'm almost thankful that your sister stole from me. That I drove that day to find you. That I'm so *blessed* to have you, Dr Parker,' he finished gruffly.

'Can I tell you I love you now?'

'Se, per favore,' he whispered urgently.

She leaned up and brushed her lips over his, then pulled back before he could take over and capture hers. *'Ti amo tanto, Alessio.'*

He swooped down and took her mouth then, every last emotion saturating their kiss until Giada was drowning in it and welcomed more.

'Chista è da me,' he breathed against her lips when they came up for air.

'Yes. I'm yours. Now and always. Now take me home, Alessio. We have a new year to welcome.'

'A new year *and* the rest of our lives,' he amended.

As she'd suspected he would.

And that was the only way she wanted it.

* * * * *

Were you enthralled by
Snowbound with the Irresistible Sicilian*?*
Then why not dive into these other fabulous
Maya Blake stories?

A Vow to Claim His Hidden Son
Their Desert Night of Scandal
His Pregnant Desert Queen
The Greek's Forgotten Marriage
Pregnant and Stolen by the Tycoon

Available now!

#4169 THE BABY HIS SECRETARY CARRIES
Bound by a Surrogate Baby
by Dani Collins

Faced with a hostile takeover, tycoon Gio must strengthen his claim on the Casella family company with a fake engagement. He'll never commit to a real one again. Despite his forbidden attraction, his dedicated PA, Molly, is ideal to play his adoring fiancée. The only problem? Molly's pregnant!

#4170 THE ITALIAN'S PREGNANT ENEMY
A Diamond in the Rough
by Maisey Yates

Billionaire Dario's electric night with his mentor's daughter Lyssia was already out-of-bounds. But six weeks later, she drops the bombshell that she's pregnant! Growing up on the streets of Rome, Dario fought for his safety, and he is determined to make his child equally safe. There is just one solution—marrying his enemy!

#4171 WEDDING NIGHT IN THE KING'S BED
by Caitlin Crews

Innocent Helene is unprepared for the wildfire that awakens at the sight of her convenient husband, King Gianluca San Felice. And she is undone by the craving that consumes them on their wedding night. But outside the royal bedchamber, Gianluca remains ice-cold—dare Helene believe their chemistry is enough to bring this powerful ruler to his knees?

#4172 THE BUMP IN THEIR FORBIDDEN REUNION
The Fast Track Billionaires' Club
by Amanda Cinelli

Former race car driver Grayson crashes Izzy's fertility appointment to reveal his late best friend's deceit before it's too late. He always desired Izzy, but their reunion unlocks something primal in Grayson. Knowing she feels it too compels the cynical billionaire to make a scandalous offer: *he'll* give her the family she wants!

#4173 HIS LAST-MINUTE DESERT QUEEN
by Annie West
Determined to save her cousin from an unwanted marriage, Miranda daringly kidnaps the groom-to-be, Sheikh Zamir. She didn't expect him to turn the tables and demand she become his queen instead—and now, he has all the power...

#4174 A VOW TO REDEEM THE GREEK
by Jackie Ashenden
The dying wish of Elena's adoptive father is to be reunited with his estranged son, Atticus. Whatever it takes, she must track down the reclusive billionaire. When she finally finds him, she's completely unprepared for the wildfire raging between them. Or for his father's unexpected demand that they marry!

#4175 AN INNOCENT'S DEAL WITH THE DEVIL
Billion-Dollar Fairy Tales
by Tara Pammi
When Yana Reddy's former stepbrother walks back into her life, his outrageous offer has her playing with fire! Nasir Hadeed will clear all her debts *if* she helps look after his daughter for three months. It's a dangerous deal—she's been burned by him before, and he remains the innocent's greatest temptation...

#4176 PLAYING THE SICILIAN'S GAME OF REVENGE
by Lorraine Hall
When Saverina Parisi discovers her engagement is part of fiancé Teo LaRosa's ruthless vendetta against her family's empire, her hurt is matched only by her need to destroy the same enemy. She'll play along and take pleasure in testing his patience. But Saverina doesn't expect their burning connection to evolve into so much more...

YOU CAN FIND MORE INFORMATION ON UPCOMING HARLEQUIN TITLES, FREE EXCERPTS AND MORE AT HARLEQUIN.COM.

HPCNMRB1223